HE WHO COMES

Reuben Cole Westerns Book 1

STUART G YATES

Copyright (C) 2020 by Stuart G. Yates

Layout design and Copyright (C) 2020 by Next Chapter

Published 2020 by Gunslinger – A Next Chapter Imprint

Edited by Fading Street Services

Cover art by Cover Mint

This book is a work of fiction. Names, characters, places, and incidents are the product of the author's imagination or are used fictitiously. Any resemblance to actual events, locales, or persons, living or dead, is purely coincidental.

All rights reserved. No part of this book may be reproduced or transmitted in any form or by any means, electronic or mechanical, including photocopying, recording, or by any information storage and retrieval system, without the author's permission.

AUTHOR'S NOTE

By 1905, when the bulk of this story is set, the use of the telephone was well established. From 1901, Brown and Son was installing telephones in schools throughout Kansas for teachers to use when wishing to contact parents. It is no distortion of history to imagine telephone use in other areas of the United States at this time.

The camera was made popular by Eastman from 1900, with his invention of the 'Brownie'. By 1905 there would be many such cameras in everyday use. Indeed, from earlier periods, we have many historically valuable images from the Old West, most markedly from the period of the Civil War.

Similarly, the idea of 'supermarkets' has to be considered as it would appear that Kestler has created such a store in this novel. The 'Piggly Wiggly' stores in which customers could purchase all their needs under one roof were not established until 1916, but Kestler's is *not* a supermarket in the truest sense of the meaning. It is a large store, providing a range of merchandise for ranchers and farmers, so it should not be confused with those large hypermarkets in which we now do the bulk of our shopping.

I hope these brief explanations add rather than detract from your enjoyment of this tale.

For Janice, who has made my life complete.

CHAPTER ONE

Reuben heard the noise that woke him in the night and thought it must be the wind taking hold of the broken yard door, which never could shut properly, causing it to bang repeatedly. Turning over, he tried to ignore it but when the noise came again, he sat bolt upright, senses straining, the dark pressing in on him like a living thing. As he waited, body coiled like a spring, he realized one very important detail: there was no wind that night. Not so much as a breath.

He sat rock still for some considerable time, mouth slightly open, heart pounding in his ears. The large, sprawling house, built by his father some fifty or so years ago when people called this piece of dirt The Wild West, seemed suddenly an unfriendly, alien place. Someone had broken in, violated his privacy. But who could it be, he wondered. This was Nineteen-hundred and five. The outlaws were all gone now. Dead, buried or forgotten. The telegraph wires hummed, cattle wandered across the plain without fear of marauding savages and he had even heard it say people had seen a horseless carriage trundling through Main Street. A German invention somebody said. Reuben Cole was not quite sure where Germany was. The modern world was as much a mystery to him.

He swung his legs out from under the blankets and waited legs bare from the knees down, his nightgown thin, shivering. Nights were cold out here. Cold and friendless. Reuben did not have many friends. He was a loner, not lone*ly,* as he was ever quick to tell anyone interested – of which there were few – but the path he had chosen kept him apart from company and he liked it that way. Nobody with whom to answer. Get up when he liked, go to bed when he liked, farted and—

There it was again. A footfall, without any mistake.

Reuben remained alert, struggling to keep his mind from freezing over. He had killed men, but that was a long time ago, out there in the open world where the questions and answers were cleaner and simpler, unlike in here, alone in the hideaway he had made for himself.

He knew he would have to go and confront whoever it was. A thief, an opportunist. Reuben had little idea how much anything in the house was worth, other than … He squeezed his eyes closed. The old painting his daddy had bought from that strange old coot over in Paris, France. The artist had died years before and his paintings, especially that large Water-Lillie one, had fetched a pretty sum. The one hanging on the dining room wall was probably worth more than the entire house.

He eased the drawer of his bedside cabinet open, careful not to make a sound, and reached inside. His hand curled around the familiar, maple wood butt of his Colt Cavalry. He took it out, gently checked the load and stood up.

He gathered himself, breathing through his mouth, eyes clamped on his bedroom door. Dawn's grey light was just beginning to find its way through the night but even so, Reuben's eyes were now well accustomed to the dark.

He took a step toward the door.

There followed an almighty crash from downstairs, so loud he almost jumped into the air. Damn it, what could that be?

Footsteps crushing shattered glass.

He knew what it was. That old Chinese thing Daddy had brought back with him from one of his many trips abroad. Ting or Ying or something. Old anyways. So big, you could plant a Love Oak inside it and still have room for an Elm.

Someone was hopping around down there, the sound unmistakable. Whoever it was must have bashed their knee against the side table holding the vase and Reuben imagined the intruder gripping his offended knee with both hands, swallowing down his curses.

The accident decided everything for him.

He tore open the door, all thoughts of maintaining silence gone. Taking the steps two at a time, he careered into the wide-open foyer and saw two men, one disappearing out the rear entrance, the other bent over, clutching his knee. He turned as Cole came in. His face turned white as ash, a soundless scream developing in his open mouth. Cole hit the man across the side of his head with the Colt, harder than he meant to, and he winced at the sound of breaking bone sounding off like a gunshot.

'Peebie? You all right in there?'

The owner of the voice came in from the dining room. Big bellied, small headed. In his hand was something that looked like a machete. Reuben shot him high up on the left shoulder, spinning him round in as fine a movement as any ballet dancer ever could complete. 'Oh, no, help,' he managed to squawk, 'he's killed *Peebie!*'

The big guy retreated before the shock of the gunshot struck home. Once he became aware he was hit, his body would shut down and he'd be as petrified as one of those fossilized trees up in Arizona Cole had read about. Blundering back into the dining room, crashing through the door, hitting the floor hard, the wounded man nevertheless managed to scramble to his feet. Reuben went after him but had not taken a single step before a grip as strong as a vice closed around his ankle. He looked down.

The dawn light, slowly but inexorably conquering the dark, bathed the original intruder in an eerie, unnatural light. Mouth open, his white teeth gnashed amongst the ruin of his cheekbone, and he gurgled, 'I'll see you in hell...'

Trying to shake him off proved useless, so Reuben put a bullet through that grinning skull and ran into the dining room in pursuit of the other one.

Something as hard and as heavy as a blacksmith's anvil hit him across the back of his head, catapulting him forward into a huge, gaping hole of blackness.

He was out cold before he hit the parquet-laminated floor.

CHAPTER TWO

Kicking off his boots, Sterling Roose stomped into his sparsely furnished office and, ignoring anything around him, went directly to the coffee pot and peered inside.

'Not the most observant of folk are you.'

Roose whirled, hand reaching for his revolver, and froze before he managed to clear the holster primarily due to it being a Remington New Model Police revolver with a five and a half inch barrel. This detail had never much bothered Roose up until now. The last time he had drawn his gun in anger had been almost twenty years earlier on that unforgettable evening when he and Reuben Cole laid out five Mexican bandits in the main drag. This, however, was not that warm, dry evening. This was a warm, dry morning and he was older, slower. Furthermore, the man sitting at his desk had a big calibre Smith and Wesson trained unerringly towards his midriff. He let his breath rattle out in a long, slow stream and straightened up. 'All right. You've made your point, stranger, now do you mind telling me what you're doing in my office?'

'The door was open.'

'That's no answer.'

'True.' The man smiled and Roose took the opportunity to study him. Clearly, he had been on the range for a prolonged period, his face swarthy with the sun, a three or four-day growth of beard not totally disguising his solid jaw, the thin mouth. Ice blue eyes twinkled from under heavy brows, and he was not young. Deep lines cut through his cheeks and around his eyes. He appeared a hardened individual, one well versed in using the gun in his hand, a hand encased in worn, kid gloves smeared, like the rest of his clothing, in the dust which invaded everything in that town. 'I'm here to talk to you about Maddie.'

'Oh.'

'Yes ... *oh*. Now, unbuckle that gun belt and sit down real slow. I have some things on my mind that you need to hear.'

'I don't even know who you are.'

'Well, that's one of the things we can discuss, now ain't it.' He waved the gun slightly. 'The gunbelt ... *real* slow.'

Things all seemed to tumble into a mess of confusion from that moment. The door burst open violently, the force almost tearing it from its hinges and Mathias Thurst, Roose's young deputy, bounded in. Wearing nothing but his sweat-stained long-johns, Thurst, like his boss, did not at first see the angular figure of the stranger sitting behind the sheriff's desk. With his arms flapping around like those of a broken windmill, he strode in, gunbelt draped over one shoulder, hat hanging by its neck cord around his throat. He wore one boot, the left one held in his left hand.

'Sheriff, oh please, you gotta come quick,' he began, his words gushing out as if from an untapped oil strike, 'It's Mrs. Samuels, she came riding in like a crazy thing on that little buggy of hers and she is telling everyone she has ...' His voice trailed away as his eyes lighted on the stranger and, in particular, the big-barreled Smith and Wesson which was now turned on him

Roose took the opportunity, swept up the small cast-iron coal shovel with which he used to keep the pot-belly stove stoked up with fuel, and with all the power he could muster, smacked it, with a good deal of satisfaction, across the stranger's jaw.

Shrieking, the stranger clutched at his right cheek and fell over the chair. Crashing to the ground, the gun skating over towards Thurst, he writhed and moaned loudly. Thurst meanwhile stooped and picked the big Smith and Wesson up. "T'ain't even loaded, Sheriff.'

Not listening, Roose nimbly darted behind his desk and cracked the shovel two or three more times across the stranger's skull. 'Swine,' he hissed. Satisfied the stranger would not be causing any more trouble, he stood up, breathing hard and glared at his young deputy. 'What was you hollerin' about, Thurst?'

It took a moment for Thurst to answer, eyes on stalks, studying the bloody and inert body of the stranger.

'*Thurst,* open your ears!'

'I ... Darn it, Sheriff, you think you might have killed him?'

'I don't care if I have,' said Roose, face flushed, sweat sprouting across his forehead. He threw the small shovel away and hoisted up his trousers. 'He was already here when I came in this morning. Had that gun on me. Don't know who he is.'

By now Thurst was next to the body, fingers pressed under the man's broken jaw. 'I don't get no pulse.'

'Thurst, can you leave it and tell me why you came in as if all the hounds of Hell were snapping at your heels.'

Thurst stood up again, shaking his head. 'Darndest thing I ever did see.' He turned to fix his gaze upon his boss. 'Mrs. Samuels, you know the one, she cleans a number of the big properties around here? Well, she went over to Reuben Cole's place and found him all beat up, just lying there in his own dining room she said.' He looked down at the body and shook his head again. 'Just like him, I guess.'

'Reuben Cole? Beat up? You sure that is what she said?'

'That's it. She's over in Drey Brewer's coffee house being comforted by them Spyrow sisters. I was on my porch when she came flying by in her buggy, pulled up real sharp and started squawking at me, almost *demanding* I come and get you. Hence my unkempt appearance, boss. I do apologize for that.'

'Don't you go fretting about any dress code, son.' He pointed at the crumpled body next to the desk. 'You, er, tidy up in here after we've put that idiot in a cell. Put his gun on my desk.'

'It's not loaded.'

'I heard you, but I wasn't to know that was I?'

'No, I guess not.'

'Well then,' Roose tugged off his jacket and flung it over the back of his chair, 'let's get him inside the jail, then I'll call on Doc Evans to fix him up.'

'He don't need no doctor, Sheriff. He needs a preacher.' Another shake of his head. 'Or Jesus, to raise him.'

CHAPTER THREE

Easing open the door to the coffee shop, Roose nodded towards Dray Brewer behind his counter, and saw Mrs. Samuels all huddled up, crying into a sodden handkerchief, two elderly and thin ladies dressed in black each with an arm around her, cooing soothing words. 'It'll be all right now, Jane, you just take your time. None of this is your fault, you've done what you can. Best leave it to the authorities now, they'll know what to do ... Oh, Sheriff Roose! A most timely intervention!'

Doffing his hat, Roose pulled up a chair and shuffled it towards the ladies. The two elderly ones made way for him, leaving the third, Jane Samuels, to regard him through eyes puffy and red with too much crying. 'Oh Sheriff, it was terrible. Poor man.'

'Is he dead?'

'No, no I am sure he isn't. I did what I could, made him comfortable, and then rushed over here as fast as I could, telling that young Thurst boy to fetch you.'

'You did the right thing, Jane,' said one of the Spyrow sisters soothingly.

'I hope so, but ... Oh, Sheriff, he has a bump the size of an egg on the back of his head.'

'Did you see who might have done it?'

'No. There were long gone, I shouldn't wonder. Whoever did it gave him a terrible beating. And the house ...' Seized by a renewed wave of anguish, she bawled into her handkerchief, 'All those lovely things that his daddy collected. So awful it is, *awful*.'

'There, there Jane, try not to upset yourself so,' said the sister closest to Roose. 'Can't you do something, Sheriff?'

'Miss Spyrow, I will do all I can to find the perpetrators, have no fear. But Mrs. Samuels, I have to ask you again. You are absolutely certain ... *is he dead?*'

Her face came up and she seemed to gather herself, taking a few shuddering breaths. Roose prepared himself for the worst. He knew Cole well. They'd ridden the range together back in the days when the Indians roamed free and tenderfoots were struggling to start a new life. He couldn't count the times Cole had saved his life, and now he too was—

'No, he's not dead, Sheriff. I told you. I tended to him, got him into bed. It was a struggle I don't mind telling you. He's a *big* man.'

'He ain't that big, but even so ...'

'Well ... I had to strip him naked, Sheriff. Bathe his bruises, so I know what I saw.'

The two sisters squealed, clamping tiny hands against their startled mouths.

Unable to hold her gaze, Roose turned away, face burning. He called across to Brewer in a shaky voice. 'Any chance of a coffee?'

The coffeehouse owner nodded, but before preparing Roose's order, he said, 'After what Mrs. Samuels said, I called across to the stable boy, Percival, to go and fetch Doctor Evans so Mr Cole could be better cared for.'

'That was good of you, Dray. Thank you.'

'I think one or two of his ribs were broken,' said Mrs. Samuels.

'I ain't never known Cole to be bettered,' Roose mused in a low voice. He swiveled in his chair and looked at the still sobbing woman. 'There must have been more than one of 'em, taken him by surprise perhaps.'

'Yes, I shouldn't wonder. There was one of those baseball bats lying beside him, with blood and bits of hair stuck to it.'

Another shriek, one of horror this time, from the accompanying sisters.

Roose contemplated this news for a moment. Most of his dealings recently had been with settlers over in the west of the county, people who were moving from the already growing cities further to the north. Some were questionable types, mainly living on the wrong side of the law, coming down from Missouri with prices on their heads. Already ideas were ruminating in his brain, suspicions mounting. If desperate men, on the brink of starvation, were beginning to reconnoitre and burglarise outlying properties, he was going to have a huge job on his hands to protect the disparate population.

'I think I might need your husband, Nelson, Mrs. Samuels. I'm going to need a good group of men to deputize. He'll be at the head of my list.'

'Nelson is too old to be going riding around searching for lowlifes, Sheriff. His army days are done.'

'Nevertheless, he was one of the ablest scouts the army ever used, and I could sure as h—' He cut off his choice of word sharply as the withering glares of the Spyrow sisters turned upon him. Squirming in his chair, he cleared his throat before he continued uneasily. 'What I mean is, he was a good scout back then, Mrs. Samuels, and the skills he had are not ones you ever forget. And he ain't old – he's two years younger than me.'

'Well, there you are, Sheriff. *Too* old by far.'

Roose returned to the sheriff's office, chewing on a cheroot, feeling he'd been dragged backwards through the sagebrush. Sweeping the floor, Thurst, bareheaded and bare-chested, glistened with sweat. He stopped sweeping as Roose came through the door and leaned on the broom, placing his chin on the end of the pole. 'Sheriff. He's dead.'

Roose felt a tightening around his gut, heartbeat accelerating, the heat of the day not helping him at all. 'That's unfortunate.'

'I'd say the way you went about him with that shovel meant there weren't ever gonna be any other result.'

'Thurst, you get on with your sweeping, then go and get yourself kitted out for an overland manhunt.'

'I'm considering not doing any of those things, Sheriff.'

'Say what?'

'The way I see it, I reckon you murdered that gentleman and I am—'

'He wasn't no gentleman, Thurst, let's get that straight right from the off. He was here to do me harm.'

'All righty, but even if he wasn't so great a guy, he's still dead and you still killed him. I think that's murder, right there and that's the truth of it, Sheriff.'

'He had a gun on me, you pond-weed.'

'An unloaded gun.'

'Like I said before, I wasn't to know that. The guy was here to kill me, that was for sure, and I wasn't about to stand around and let him do it. If you hadn't burst in on us it would be me setting out my patch in the cemetery, not him.'

Mathias Thurst stood staring, not at Roose, but into the jail beyond and the bundled up heap that once was a man. Roose followed his deputy's eyes and considered his options. What would he have done if Thurst hadn't arrived at that most convenient of times, he wondered. What did the man have to say about Maddie or anything else for that matter? Surely sure the man was Maddie's husband. Roose had been more than friendly with the man's wife for some time. Of course, Roose knew Maddie was married, but he believed it was all over between them, so what had galvanized her husband into a confrontation he could not say. Clearly, he needed a little face-to-face with his lover of over six months, to bring some light to the situation. Right now, however, he had other, more pressing worries, Thurst being the main one.

Roose blew out his cheeks and measured his deputy with a cold look, hands on hips, well away from the New Model

Police sitting in its holster, set ready for a cross-belly draw. 'Mathias, we can work all this out, we truly can, but at the moment we have got a manhunt to get started. I aim to find those responsible for breaking into Cole's home and beating him close to death. I will need you.'

'I ain't going,' said Thurst without pausing for a moment to consider Roose's words. 'I'm done with this and done with you, Sheriff.'

'Now hold on just a minute there, Thurst, this isn't all about you and me! We can deal with this when we get back.'

'How will we do that?'

'Well, I'll make a sworn statement ... Present it to the circuit judge. You can witness it or even give your own account of what happened.'

'After we get back from the manhunt?'

'Yes! That's exactly right. This unfortunate incident will keep – it's not as if he's going anywhere is it?'

'And what if I don't come back?'

'What if you don't ... What are you talking about? Of course, you'll come back!'

'What I mean is, what if I was to be the victim of an accident, a stray bullet, a rattler sliding underneath my blankets? What then, Sheriff? It would just be your word and ...' He chuckled, a strangely humourless and eerie sound in that small, dusty room. 'Nobody would ever question any of it, would they, you being such an upright citizen and all.'

'What do you take me for, Thurst? I'm as law-abiding as anyone.'

'Why you set to him the way you did?'

'Listen, it's complicated all right. He's Maddie's husband – *was* Maddie's husband.'

'So that's why you killed him?'

'Thurst, you've got this all wrong! I was acting in self-defence.'

Thurst turned away, setting the broom against the side of the pot-belly stove. 'Well, I've made my mind up. I ain't going. I'll stay here until you get back, hold the fort so to speak. And I'll do something with the body – it is liable to get somewhat ripe in this heat.'

'Thurst, there is no need to—'

'There is every need Sheriff. I ain't dumb and I ain't gonna risk my life because you killed a man.'

And that was that. Roose could see it in his deputy's eyes. He was not going to be persuaded, one way or the other. Roose let his shoulders relax and strode forward, pushing past Thurst. He pulled down three Winchesters from the open cabinet and stuffed his pockets with cartridges. 'I'm taking Samuels with me and probably Ryan Stone too. Both of 'em served in the army and they know what it is like to be out on the open-range.' He stacked the Winchesters into the crook of his arm and glared at his deputy. 'You've let me down, Mathias. When we get back, we'll sort this out. And it won't be to your advantage.'

'At least I'll still be alive.'

Roose went to say something, thought better of it and stomped outside into the glaring heat of yet another airless day.

CHAPTER FOUR

They rode sluggishly across the endless plain, all three men wearing broad-brimmed Mexican sombreros. Hunched over their scrawny mounts, whose own legs buckled under the weight of their riders, the relentless heat drained all strength and made even the most simple of physical actions an epic in determination and effort. The lead man was huge and rode a mule. Against each of the animal's flanks banged and clanged bulging canvas bags, the noise from which reverberated across the scorching landscape, a landscape bereft of shade.

'Soloman,' said the second in line, his voice weak and scratchy, 'we have to find a spot to rest, if not for us then the horses.'

Solomon rolled his huge shoulders, pulled off his hat, and dragged a sleeve across his brow. He was bald save for a few wisps of oily black hair, which he had once, some while ago, swept over his pate in an attempt to disguise his lack of anything on top. It hadn't worked and he had given up the struggle and surrendered to the inevitable. Compared to his bulk, the head was so small people called him 'pin-head', but never to his face. Such a thing would be suicidal, for Soloman was a man well versed in killing. It was something he enjoyed.

He reined in his mule. The animal, when it decided it wanted to, slowed to almost stopping, but not quite. 'I ain't too sure where any of that shade might be, Pete.'

Pete came up alongside him. The sweat rolled down his face, cutting tiny rivulets through the grime covering every inch of him. 'We should never have come this way. We should have taken the trail. It's known to us and we—'

'They'd have caught up with us.'

'*Who*? Sheriff Roose? It would be hours, maybe even days before he worked out what had happened.'

'Well, I wasn't taking no chances.'

'That was Reuben Cole,' said the third man, bringing his horse alongside the other side of Solomon. 'I saw the portrait of his daddy above the fireplace before I put my Bowie through it.'

'Reuben-whoever-he-was is dead,' said Solomon with feeling. He recalled the deep, almost sexual satisfaction he derived from slamming his boot into the man's ribcage.

'You don't know that for sure,' said Pete.

Turning in the saddle, Solomon gave Pete a withering glare. 'I beat him real good, Pete. No one could survive the beating I gave that piece of bar-filth.'

'Yeah, so you say, Sollo, but we don't know that for s—'

'*I* know it. I ain't never been bettered in no fight and not many have ever got up again after taking a beating from me. He's the same. He's *dead*, I tell you – D-E-D, dead!'

'Well, that makes the case for Roose coming after us even more definite, don't it?' The others looked at the third man. Pencil-thin, his face, hands and any other piece of exposed flesh were burnt almost to a crisp, every patch of his clothing, both covering his torso and his legs, soaked through with sweat. 'What?'

'You don't have to state the obvious, Notch.,' said Pete, 'we all know what Roose will do.'

'Yeah, but like I say,' put in Solomon, turning his eyes to the distant horizon and the mass of dry grey scree that divided them from it, 'he won't discover the body for days. We have plenty of time to make it to Lawrenceville and deliver this here booty to Mr Kestler. It'll be a payday like no other.'

'If we ever make it,' said Notch, shaking his water canteen for grim effect. The sound of a few dregs of liquid splashed around inside. 'I ain't barely got a mouthful left in here.'

'Me neither,' said Pete, downcast.

'Will you two stop squawking! Lawrenceville cannot be more than half a day's ride away, so we are not going to die from thirst out here.' He gingerly dipped his right hand under his filthy shirt to feel the pulsating wound where Cole had shot him. The bullet had gone clean through. 'I always was lucky when it comes to getting shot, but this hurts like sin.' He looked at his bloody fingers and licked them.

'I hope you is right about us not dying out here, Sollo,' groaned Pete, head hanging further down onto his chest, voice sounding defeated.

'I am right, damn you, Pete! You ain't been shot but all you do is moan like some old woman. Now buck up and let's continue before we really do fry out here.'

With that, Solomon kicked the mule's flanks several times. Eventually, it moved a little faster, but not by much. It plodded across the hard, arid ground where nothing grew, everything covered in a uniform grey dust which reflected the glare of the sun's rays, bouncing them back into the faces of both men and beasts. Solomon pulled off his neckerchief and covered most of his face with it and, to give further relief from the brightness, pull his sombrero down as far as he could without causing it to fall off. In this way, he could protect himself from the scorching glare as much as possible. The others followed his example, set their shoulders, and continued, resigned to what they had to do. Too far to go back the way they had come, there was no other choice but to follow Soloman's lead.

It may have been two hours later, although it probably felt like two *days* when Pete thought he heard something, reined in his horse and strained to listen.

There! Beyond the distant crest, the sound of …

Narrowing his eyes, he saw it, stark against the white sky. A trail of grey trailing backwards from its point of origin. Not a fire. Smoke. 'Smoke by Jiminy! *Smoke!*'

The others reacted, Soloman the first to do so, jumping down from his mule when it refused to come to a total standstill. 'Darn it, wish I had me a telescope. Smoke you say?'

'No mistaking it,' cried Pete, unable and unwilling to keep the triumph out of his voice.

'Maybe it's Injuns,' said Notch forlornly. 'They send smoke signals, don't they?'

'No it ain't Indians, that's the railroad,' said Soloman, spinning around and throwing his sombrero high into the air. 'The railroad to Lawrenceville! Boys, we is saved!'

The others gawped at him but they knew it was true.

They were saved.

CHAPTER FIVE

Roose came out of Doc Evans' home, which doubled as his surgery and stood on the porch, looking down the street towards a voice he recognized.

It was Maddie. Dressed in a cornflower blue dress, with a tiny pillbox hat set upon her mass of tumbling golden locks, she drove a small buggy, calling, 'Sterling, what in blazes is going on?'

One of the things he truly adored about Maddie was the way her beautiful looks did not quite match the coarse sounding voice. She was a wildcat, both in and out of bed, and he smiled with a mixture of pride and joy as she drew closer. She was as hard as they come while always managing to look as pretty as a picture.

However, in her eyes today burned something he did not recognize.

She pulled up close and yanked back the wheel brake. Studying him for a few moments, her voice cracked as she spoke. "I went to your office to call in on you being as you left me without a word this morning.'

'Ah, yes, I'm sorry about that but—'

'And when I got there, your young deputy and another youth is manhandling a body out of the cell. So I stops, all of a flutter as you would expect,' – he did and he pulled off his hat and went to explain but was intercepted yet again – 'when I look and see who it was.'

'Who it … Well, I have to admit he did mention you by name so I assumed he was a jealous lover.' The lie came easily to him, for he knew full well the dead man was her husband but he couldn't tell her that. Roose shot her a coy smile. 'I am well aware you have several other gentlemen friends.'

'He was *more* than a friend, Sterling! It was Gunther.'

'Gunther?'

'Yes, you dimwit – Gunther Haas, *my husband*!'

For one terrible moment, Roose believed he could be in danger of over-acting as his mouth opened and his eyes bulged. Gaping grotesquely, he forced a strained, 'Husband?' She nodded and, to give her words more emphasis, she sniffed loudly, produced a silk handkerchief from her sleeve and blew her nose into it. Roose ran a shaking hand across his mouth. 'Oh jeepers.'

'Yes, you may well say 'oh jeepers'!' She gave her nose another blast then climbed down from the buggy seat and stepped up to him, hands on her hips, head tilted, mouth set in a thin line. 'You seriously telling me you didn't know who he was?'

'I swear it.'

'All right, if that is so, you tell me what Gunther is doing in *your* jail, dead as a post.'

Hearing the raised voices and Maddie's heartfelt sobbing, Doc Evans stepped from out of his surgery, assessed the situation, and helped Maddie inside. He set her down at his kitchen table while Roose, following like a chastised dog, stood in the doorway, arms folded, wondering how he was going to survive the next few minutes.

'There, there, Mrs. Haas,' said the Doc in soothing tones as he set a glass of water down before her, 'try and drink that and don't upset yourself so.'

Mumbling her thanks, Maddie did as suggested. She sat quietly, dabbing at her eyes and nose with the handkerchief, inhaled breath shuddering in her throat.

Turning from her, Doc Evans' eyes settled on Roose, the unspoken question hanging there.

"She's had some bad news,' said Roose, unable to hold the doctor's stare. 'Very bad.'

'He's *dead,* damn your eyes, Sterling Roose!'

Turning from one to the other, a deep frown forming ever more pronounced, Evans shook his head. 'Who is dead?'

'Her husband.'

Evans gaped and looked at Maddie, whimpering. 'Your husband? Why I never even knew he was back in town. How long is it since you—'

'Over three years.'

'Well, I'll be.' Shaking his head, Doc Evans went over to a large, glass-fronted cabinet, opened it and carefully extracted a bell jar bottle, about three-quarters full of a brown liquid. He pulled out the stopper and filled a small glass from the bottle and handed it over to Maddie. 'Medicinal brandy. I'm guessing you could do with that right now.'

She nodded her thanks, paused for a moment, then tipped the contents of the glass straight down her throat.

Evans gave Roose a startled look, Roose responding with a slight shrug and a knowing raising of the brows.

'Thank you, Doctor,' she said, thrusting out the glass towards Evans. 'Another if you don't mind.'

Roose suppressed a chuckle as Evans poured out a second healthy measure. Maddie took her time with this one.

'I'm sincerely sorry for your loss. I shall ask Miss Coulson, my nurse, to accompany you home. You shouldn't be alone after such a shock.' He turned to Roose. 'I'm assuming there was foul play, so any idea who might have done such a thing?'

'Oh yes,' said Roose with a slight smile, 'I have a very good idea.'

Maddie refused the offer of being accompanied home. Instead, she got Roose to steer the little buggy out of the town limits and bring it to a halt on the top of a nearby knoll, under the shade of several trees.

'You killed him, didn't you?'

'Now why would you think such a thing?'

'Because I saw the look in your eyes when the good doctor asked you.'

Roose cleared his throat, taking out his tobacco pouch. 'I had no idea he was your husband.'

'Would that have made any difference?'

'Maybe, Maybe not,' he drizzled a line of tobacco onto a paper and deftly rolled it into shape. 'He had a gun on me, was most likely set on shooting me dead. I did what I had to do.' He studied her. 'How come you never mentioned him all the times we've been together?'

'We were estranged.'

'E-what?'

'Estranged. Separated. He'd started playing around with some Mexican harlot called Beatriz Gomez a few years back so I threw him out. Best thing I ever did. It was always my intention to tell you, Sterling ...' A fluttering of the eyelashes. 'I promise.'

'Bah, it don't much matter to me none.' He put the cigarette into his mouth, struck a lucifer on the dull metal tin in which he kept his papers, and touched the flame to the end. It flared and Roose took in a pull of smoke and blew it out in a long stream. 'What's done is done. I have more important things to think about. And I need your ranch hand to help me out.'

'Cougan? He's a live one, that man is just like his pa.'

'I knew his pa. Knew him well.'

'Then you'll know his son still blames us all for what happened to his family down in Louisiana. They were hanged, fleeing from the plantation there were all working on. He doesn't take too kindly to white folks, especially the law-making kind.'

'I don't make the law, Maddie, I just dish out its justice. Reuben Cole was beaten half to death by a bunch of drifters last ni—' He stopped when he saw her face, those eyes widening, lips trembling. For a moment it seemed to him she was about to faint. 'Are you all right?'

Taking a moment, she pulled out a small silk handkerchief from her sleeve and dabbed it at her mouth. 'Cole? Is he ... I mean, beaten half to death you said.'

'Yeah ...' He swept his eyes over her. If he wasn't mistaken she seemed more disturbed by the news about Cole than she had about her husband. 'But you know Cole ...' A look of alarm ran across her features.

'Well, *yes*, I know him, but not in that way, Sterling.'

'I never said you did, Maddie,' Roose said slowly, eyes locked on hers now. 'What I meant was, he is as tough as they come and they may have tried their darndest, but they didn't succeed in killing him.'

'Ah yes, yes of course.' She forced a tiny chuckle and returned the handkerchief to its resting place. 'So, what happened exactly?'

'They broke into his house and have run off with almost all of his family heirlooms, probably worth a goodly sum, and I aim to bring 'em back to pay their dues.'

'Yes. Yes, of course ... But why do you need Cougan?'

'Because he is one of the best local shootin' men and I might have need of his services. I have a couple of trackers, but I doubt they'll be much good in a firefight.' He laughed as he studied the burning end of his cigarette. 'Fortuitous of you to come into town when you did. Perhaps it's a sign.'

She sniffed loudly, emotions recovering. 'Poor Gunther. You had no need to kill him.'

'I had every need. He would have killed me.'

'Well, we'll see what the judge has to say about that.'

'Judge? What what do you mean by that?'

'I *mean* I aim to let justice take its course, Sterling. I'm only repeating your own sentiments on the matter.'

'You are a vixen, Maddie! I told you I had no choice.'

'We shall see. There are bound to be witnesses.'

'What? Who have you spoken to? Whoever it was, they have got it wrong, I swear to you.'

'No Sterling, I haven't spoken to anyone, not yet. But I think I might have a fair idea where to start.' She smiled. 'Now, if you're not going to kiss me, take yourself back into town and then you can get on with your manhunt.'

They waited until late in the afternoon before they spotted Cougan coming into town astride of a large and powerful looking colt. He was a large, heavily muscled man, who wore a grey army shirt, and army blue pants held up by broad braces. In his waistbelt was a Navy Colt and, in its sheath slapping against the horse's rump, a Spencer carbine. If it wasn't for the ridiculously small bowler set askew on top of his close-shaven pate, he looked for all the world like a man on a mission.

'Dear Lord, he is one big bruiser,' said Nelson Samuels, waiting on his own horse next to Roose.

'He is a fister,' said Roose, 'so try not to rile him too much.' He looked askew at the other man he had pressed into service, Ryan Stone, a tall, wiry-looking man with sharp features. He looked mean and Roose felt a knot tightening in his middle. 'You're not looking too pleased with our companion's arrival, Ryan. Why's that? Had dealings with Cougan before?'

'Our paths have crossed.' He leaned over the side of his horse, hawked and spat into the dirt. 'Never did like him. A loud-mouthed boaster is what he is. What possessed you to bring him along?'

'He's the finest shot this side of the Mississippi. No other reason. See that big old Sharps he's lugging? He can take a rattler's eye out at a thousand yards with it.'

'That's a Spencer carbine, Sheriff,' said Samuels slowly. 'Not that it matters if he can use it.' Samuels shifted his weight in his saddle. 'Let's just do the niceties and get this thing done. My wife is all shook-up because of Reuben Cole and she wants those men apprehended.'

'Or killed,' muttered Ryan, his eyes never leaving Cougan as the big man reined in not half a dozen paces from them. He did not speak.

Roose didn't either, giving Cougan the briefest of nods before turning his mount around and kicking it into a lazy trot. Thinking things through, he wouldn't mind at all if those men were killed. Killing had always been something of a bedfellow for Sterling Roose.

CHAPTER SIX

They left Fort Concho in the late August of Eighteen-seventy-four. The orders were despatched some days previously and Reuben Cole, together with Sterling Roose, stood outside the main entrance to their barracks on the evening prior to their departure, smoking and gazing out towards the vast prairie surrounding them.

'Heard it's about Comanch,' said Reuben, letting the smoke stream from between his lips. He was not a great smoker, allowing himself one in the evening before he settled down to sleep. "Again," he added, unable to keep the bitterness out of his voice.

'Heard a bunch of Cheynee and Arapaho have joined 'em. Broke out the reservation to follow a band of Kiowa. There's a lot of 'em, maybe two thousand.'

'If that's true, we're in for a long ol' haul this time, Sterling.'

'It's always a long ol' haul when it comes to Comanch. They don't take prisoners. And this time, according to the Colonel, neither do we. The government want 'em back in that reservation and we are to do whatever is necessary to succeed in that demand.'

'You know a lot about this, don't you?'

A mischievous glint played around Roose's eyes. 'To tell you the truth, Rube, I was listening at Colonel Mackenzie's door after I saw that express rider come blazing across the parade ground. A few of us crept across and listened to what he had to say.'

'That was brave of you. If Sergeant Dixon had found you he'd have—'

'Shoot, Rube, Dixon was the first one over there.' He chuckled. 'I'm guessing he was hoping for an easy retirement. His wife's expecting their first.'

'Maybe he'll get compassionate leave.'

'Against Comanches? Are you kidding me? No, they need every one of us out there, to push 'em up against the Red River, causing them as much hardship as possible and so force 'em back where they came from. But Lone Wolf is leading 'em and he is as hard as the mountains which hem us in from every side. He won't go down without a fight.'

As they streamed out of the main entrance, with Reuben and Roose at the van, the sun blazed overhead, beating down with an intensity that was almost too harsh to bear. As scouts, they wore broad-brimmed straw hats and buckskin clothes which afforded some protection. Ben Cougan, the third scout, had brought himself a parasol which he now twirled daintily between his sausage-thick fingers. 'Got me this from a young whore down in El Paso. Best thing she ever gave me – she was as ugly as an old coot.'

'So says the Greek Adonis,' chuckled Roose.

'What was that you said?'

'Nothing Ben,' said Roose with a grin, 'only commenting on your supreme good looks and how you can charm the prettiest of young things into your bed.' He winked.

Cougan glared, not believing a word of it. He was a dangerous, unpredictable individual, but Reuben had knocked him on his backside on more than one occasion, and said simply, 'Leave it, Ben.' That was enough.

The undulating landscape was an arid, broken plain, the compacted earth punctuated with clusters of rocks and clumps of sage. An acrid smell caught at the back of men's throats and the three scouts pulled up their bandanas to cover nose and mouth.

They set a steady pace, threading their mounts through the rough ground, knowing the most dangerous thing to do out here would be for a horse to turn an ankle in a hidden depression. The occasional rattler hissed its warning and sometimes the rare sight of a soaring eagle caused them to look skywards. Apart from these nothing else stirred and the only sounds were the plodding of hooves and the groans of cavalrymen close to the edge of boredom.

'I don't like this,' said the young second-in-command, Lieutenant Nathan Brent, fresh-faced and immaculately turned out despite the heat. He'd ridden up to the scouts who walked some hundred paces ahead of the column.

Roose, leaning forward, hands on the pommel of his saddle, gave him an encouraging look, liking his eagerness and his innocence. 'What exactly don't you like, Lieutenant?'

'Look at it,' he swept his arm dramatically in a wide arc, 'we're too open. Commanches could be hiding in a gulley, just waiting to attack.'

'Hit and run, you mean?' interjected Cole.

'Yes! Precisely.'

'What do you suggest, Lieutenant?' asked Roose, stretching out his back. 'We could spread out, but I don't believe there are any Indians out here.'

'They're more likely to be hiding amongst those rocks,' said Cole, pointing towards a distant range of low jagged mountains, which sprouted from the grey earth like giants' teeth. 'The summits are virtually unscaleable, but there's a whole system of caves, crags and hidden pathways where any number of men could hide.'

'Then we should check them out, seeing as we are heading in that direction.'

Cole looked uncomfortable and gave Roose a look.

'That's a good two-hour ride, Lieutenant. We wouldn't be back until nightfall.' He looked around, reached inside one of his saddlebags and pulled out a pair of German, precision-built binoculars. He scanned the plain over to his left, grunting when he found what he was looking for. 'Yonder is a small knot of trees and gorse, which will provide the horses with a little relief from the sun. My advice would be to make camp there and await our return.' He continued to swing the glasses to cover every direction.

'And post pickets,' said Cole. 'Your very best men.'

The three scouts rode at a fair pace across the flat earth, setting a course least sprinkled with broken rock fragments. As they drew closer to the base of the mountains, the scree increased dramatically, forcing them to skirt to the east as they searched for a way into the mountain network.

Giving way to a large depression, the landscape changed suddenly, with grassland and small areas of woodland replacing the uniform greyness of the plain. It was here they spotted a small cluster of timber buildings. Reining in, Roose again brought his binoculars to his eyes. 'All righty, we have here a cabin. It appears well built, and recent, with a fenced in area to the rear. Probably vegetables and the like. There's a small barn and a stable but I can't see any horses ... There's a well, and to ...'

His voice trailed away as he slowly lowered the field glasses and turned to face Cole who sat, waiting in silence.

'What?'

'There's something behind the well ...' He put the glasses to his eyes, adjusting the focus ring slightly. 'It looks ... I can't quite make it out as it's obscured by the well ...'

'Let's go down there,' said Cougan, pausing for a moment to spit over his horse's neck. 'There ain't nothing moving for a hundred square miles in this dead and dying land. Look at it – nothing grows except twisted gorse bushes and the like. Why would anyone live out here?'

'They have worked hard, whoever they are,' said Roose, continuing to scan the settlement, 'they have planted a good deal of wheat. Real farmers, not eager amateurs. Look at those fields, that ain't the work of someone who doesn't know what they're doing.'

'So where are they?'

Roose lowered the glasses again and answered his friend's question with a simple shrug.

'I'm going down there,' said Cougan as he deftly collapsed the parasol and placed it just behind the saddle pommel. 'The longer we sit out here the more likely we is to get fried. Besides, they might have some grub, a good cup of coffee, wholesome bread.' Licking his lips, his patted his ample stomach, reached behind him and pulled out his Spencer carbine from its sheath. 'You comin'?'

'I don't like it,' said Roose. 'It looks well tended and all, but why is there no one about?'

'Maybe they're inside, eating.' Cougan kicked his horse's flanks and set off down the slight incline. I'll go take a look-see.' Soon he was cutting a trail through the grass.

'We follow him?'

'Nope,' said Cole. 'We go in from the flanks. You take the right. Sweep round in a wide arc and when you come through the other side of the grass, dismount and move in slow.'

'You expecting trouble?'

'I don't know what to expect,' said Cole, checking his Winchester with deliberate care, 'but something is not right. All the horses gone, that causes me a good deal of concern, Sterling, I'll tell you that much.' He took a long drink from his water canteen and eased himself from the saddle. 'I´ll go in on foot. If you hear shootin', forget what I said about moving slowly and ride in hard and fast.'

Chewing on his bottom lip, Roose took one final sweep with the binoculars, shook his head, and cantered away to the far side.

CHAPTER SEVEN

Groaning with the effort, Cole sat up in bed as Maddie came into the room. Head tilted, she studied him disdainfully with pursed lips and jutting chin. 'Just look at you, Cole.'

'Good mornin' to you too, Maddie.'

He struggled to make himself more comfortable, grunting and groaning, trying to find the best position. She came up close, pulling him to her as she puffed up one of the three pillows behind his back, before easing him gently against the now well-padded headboard. 'You look like you need a helping hand.'

'Anything from you would help just fine.'

She stepped back, brushing away a strand of hair from his forehead. 'Don't let Sterling hear you talking like that.'

'When are we going to tell him?'

Maddie made a face, shot her head towards the bedroom door then back again. 'Sssh, you fool! He's just outside, talking to the others. He'll be here in a minute.'

'Answer my question.'

'Not now, you idiot! Earlier, when he told me about what had happened, I think he suspected something.'

'Why would he do that?'

'Damn it, Cole! Are you actually stupid, or what? Because of my reaction to what they did to you. I almost broke down with worry.'

'There's no need to worry about me, Maddie. I've had a lot worse, believe me. So, what did he say?'

'Nothing, thank the Lord. I think I managed to divert his attention when I told him I'd be reporting what happened to Gunther to the judge.'

'Gunther? You mean he's back?'

Taking her time, checking and rechecking the door as she did so, she told Cole about what had happened in the jailhouse. He listened without comment and when she'd finished, she smoothed out the blankets over his chest. 'Anyways, he's all set to go riding through the prairie looking for the men that did this to you. I mean, *look* at you, Reuben!' For the first time, tears appeared under her bottom eyelids, and a tiny trail spilt down over her cheek. 'Darn it, I didn't want to cry, but ... *damn you, Reuben!*'

He reached out to her as her fists bunched and seized both her arms. She gasped. 'It wasn't my fault, Maddie! They came in the night, looking to steal whatever they could. Broke two or three of Pa's finest things. I shot and killed one of them, but the other did for me as he hid behind the door. I guess I wasn't thinking so straight.'

'When do you ever?'

'I am with you, Maddie. I'm in love with you.'

She stopped, the colour as well as the tension falling from her face. For a moment it seemed to Cole she was about to cry again. He went to speak but before he could say anything more, she recovered and tore herself from his grip. 'What do you know about love, Reuben? You've spent half your life on the trail, the other half moping about in this great big empty house of yours.'

'Until you came along.'

'*Until I* ... Reuben, we've spent a few brief moments together.'

'And in those moments I've realised just how much I need you.'

Her eyes sparkled with a mix of surprise, sadness and something else ... He wished it was hope. A shared desire to be together. He'd felt it as she lay in his arms the last time they were together. The way she'd snuggled into him, her voice so soft, so sweet. He knew what they had transcended mere physicality. Now, with that wide-eyed expression, he could see it again.

She went to speak then caught her breath as the sound of approaching footsteps made all further conversation impossible.

'Well, well, there's a pretty picture.'

It was Roose, framed in the doorway, hat tilted to one side, thumbs in his gunbelt. Maddie, swivelling around and giggled, which sounded to Cole forced, false. If Roose picked up on it, he neither said so nor changed position. 'Sterling, you are a dumb ass,' Maddie said. 'I'm only here giving Reuben my comfort, which is more than you're doing. I mean *look* at him.'

Pushing himself from the doorframe, Roose strode forward, the sound of his boots ominous in that small, dark room. 'Let some light in,' he said, rolling himself a cigarette.

Maddie quickly went over to the main window and opened up the shutters. Instantly, rays of sunlight streamed in, picking out the haze of dust hanging in the air. 'My, this place needs a good clean,' she said.

Roose grinned at his old friend. 'It's true what she says, Reubs – you do look all beat up.'

Unconsciously, Cole felt the swelling around his jaw. The worst of the pain was across his ribs where they'd laid into him with their boots. He didn't feel it at the time, having had the back of his skull cracked open like an egg. The bandages he wore were caked in dried blood. 'I might have to shave my head to get this thing off,' he said, prodding at the lint dressing.

'Leave it,' snapped Maddie, slapping away his hand. 'Have you no sense? The doctor said to rest, so rest.'

'She's right,' said Roose, lighting up his cigarette. He blew out a long stream. 'I have three good men waiting outside. We aim to ride out and pick up their trail. We have a witness who said they saw three men high-tailed it north-west. The only town within a hundred miles of north-west is Lawrenceville.'

'That ain't the most welcoming of towns, you know that.'

'It's still pretty much lawless. But the railroad arrived two years ago so things are bound to have improved. A man called Kestler is the constable there.'

'You know him?'

'Know *of* him. Heard a few things. Not all of them complimentary.'

Reuben made to throw back the blanket covering him, but Maddie was there first, 'What do you think you're doing, Reuben Cole?'

He laughed. 'I'm getting up, putting my boots on and going with them.'

'No you ain't,' said Roose quickly, acknowledging Maddie's wild, pleading look. 'You'd only hold us up.'

'You know that's not true. I'm the best-darned tracker in this whole county.'

'That you are, but you're in no shape to help. I can handle it.'

'Yeah, I'm sure you can, but with me riding alongside you, we'd handle it a lot better.'

Roose let out a blast of smoke. 'No, Reuben. I can't take the risk. The doc said—'

'That's right, Reuben,' cut in Maddie, 'the doc said you have to rest, that you can't take the risk of opening that head-wound up again. You need to *mend*, Reuben.'

'Maddie,' said Cole, doing his best to keep his temper, 'why don't you go outside for a moment, make sure those other boys have their canteens well filled with water.' She glared at him. 'Please, Maddie.'

She gave up the fight. Not looking too pleased with any of it, she stormed out, her long dress sweeping across the floor, sending up more clouds of dust.

Watching her go, Roose turned to consider his friend. 'She seems mighty concerned with you, Reubs.'

'She always has had a soft-spot.'

Nodding, Roose threw down his finished smoke and ground it with his boot. 'As far as I was aware, you don't know each other that well.'

'Well, that's true, Sterling. Dang it, are you jealous or something?'

'Jealous? No. Why, should I be?'

'Not at all, old friend.'

'Well, that's all right then.' He readjusted his belt. 'I aim to bring those varments to justice, Cole. You can count on me.'

'I know I can. This isn't about your abilities. You know that.'

'Remember back in Seventy-four when we rode across the great plain with Cougan.'

'Oh Lordy, why you thinking of that?'

'I don't know. It came to me the other day, the memory. So clear. Almost as if I was re-living it.'

'Well, you sure as anything don't want to do that.'

'I know, but …' He heaved in a deep breath and sat down on the bed next to his old friend. 'These thieves, they've taken almost the self-same route. It got me to thinking, that's all.'

'Thinking about those times, Sterling …' He shook his head. 'They're not dreams, they is nightmares.'

'Got a report come in across the wire. A whisper, to be honest. A group of Comanch have broken out again.'

'What?' Cole sat up, ignoring the pain, but gritting his teeth nevertheless. 'How many?'

'I don't know. Half a dozen. Some youngster's been whipping up things, getting some of the old boys agitated. They robbed a bank in a little town about fifty miles out of El Paso. Killed two tellers and wounded a young woman.' He looked into Cole's eyes. 'A pregnant woman. She's lost the baby.'

Snapping his head away, Cole bit down on his bottom lip. 'This ain't *ever* gonna end.'

'There's a chance we will come across 'em as we chase down the others. If we do ...' He leaned forward. 'Cole. You remember back then when we found that deserted house?'

Cole grunted, nodded his head once.

'You remember how we went in? You remember what we found?'

'What is it you're trying to say, Sterling?'

'I'm not sure I could go through that again.'

'It's haunting you, ain't it?' Roose nodded, not able to look his friend in the face any longer. 'Then let's talk it out and banish those ghosts forever.'

CHAPTER EIGHT

The memories returned, as vivid as if they were from yesterday. Cole listened intensely, all discomfort forgotten as Roose returned to that moment thirty years ago when they came upon a deserted homestead.

Roose took a wide berth, keeping the pace of his horse steady, using the long grass as partial cover from anyone who might be watching from the cabin. From a distance of around two to three hundred yards, he kept the settlement in plain view, stopping every so often to train his German-made precision field glasses on the cluster of buildings. He saw Cougan striding through the grass, rifle in hands. From twenty paces away, the big man had dismounted and now marched defiantly on, going straight through the open door of the cabin, paying no mind to the bundle behind the well. Intrigued, Roose once more focused in on what appeared to be a pile of clothes.

Until he saw the naked arm.

He dropped the glasses from his grip and kicked his horse into a canter, cutting a wide swathe through the gentle swaying grass, stirred by a hot breeze blowing in across the fields.

A shout, more of a strangulated bark, and Cougan appeared in the cabin entrance, staggering like a drunkard, his hands empty, the rifle gone. Roose turned his horse and jumped down at the run, levering his carbine, dropping to his knees when within calling range and training the weapon on the door.

'Cougan?' He waited, either for his companion to move or say something. There was no discernable reaction, however, only the swaying from side to side. Cougan's face, ashen-grey, seemed to have turned to stone, mouth and eyes wide open, but no life there. He was, Roose mused with chilling certainty, like a ghost. Already dead.

Something moved beyond the bulk of the inert Cougan. A shape, a man perhaps. Roose fired a single round into the blackness of the cabin, the large calibre bullet streaking over Cougan's left shoulder. A muffled cry followed by silence.

'Cougan?' Roose hissed again. More urgent now, as he levered another round into the Spencer and cocked the hammer. He sucked in a breath and steadied himself. Waiting, always the hardest part when shooting, Roose listened out for any sound of movement from within.

There was nothing.

Keeping low, Cole approached the side of the cabin from the mountainside. He dropped to his belly some dozen paces or so and slithered forward. The bundle of clothing behind the well caught his eye and from this angle and distance, he could clearly see it was a body. A young woman, contorted in the unmistakable pose of death.

Cougan came out of the doorway and stood swaying like a willow. Cole rolled away, deciding to take the rear of the cabin. Reaching the corner, he got to his haunches and checked his Winchester. He was about to move when the boom of Roose's carbine brought him up short and he waited, mouth open, straining to hear anything.

A low groan from inside the timber building. Definitely a man, possibly badly hurt.

Or possibly also a trick, to lure Roose indoors.

Taking a few urgent breaths, Cole chanced a look around the corner.

There was a man, kneeling in the stable doorway on the other side of the rear yard. Cole darted away again behind the cover of the cabin wall. He waited, eyes squeezed shut, recalling the man's look. Long hair, blue shirt, buckskin pants. An Indian, possible Comanche or Kiowa. He chanced another look.

Beyond the yard fence, they were taking the horses away at a gallop. Perhaps half a dozen men, some doubled up on their own mounts, leading the roped together animals across the far fields, kicking up a lot of dust as there the grass was not in such lush condition. Perhaps the settlers, or farmers more like, had left it fallow for the following season. Cole clamped his mouth shut. They'd never be farming this land again.

He chanced another look towards the stable. There were two of them now and, as yet, they hadn't spotted him, so he dipped back, flattened himself against the wall and bided his time. As soon as they broke cover, he too would move.

He had no way of knowing how many more renegades were lurking amongst the settlement. He'd estimated at least six of them making off with the retreating horses. Reports had said around a dozen Indians had broken free from the reservation, so somewhere milling around were a further six warriors. If Roose had hit one in the cabin, there were still five or so more to contend with.

Cole pressed the Winchester against his chest and measured his breathing. Comanche and Kiowas were just about the best for moving silently. They could already have made the rear entrance to the cabin.

So, sucking in a deep breath, he moved.

With no subsequent movement or sound emanating from inside the cabin, Roose decided to lower his carbine. Cougan continued to maintain his curious swaying motion, but Roose felt that almost certainly the man was dead. His big body leaned against the door frame, the only thing to prop him up. But it was the man's missing rifle that worried Roose the most.

Head down, he broke cover and ran half-crouched to the well, throwing himself up against its curved wall. From this angle, he had perfect cover to protect himself from anyone in the cabin shooting at him. Not from the stable, however.

There were two men in the open doorway and they were running also.

As they ran, another man appeared in the stable entrance, covering them with a partially-drawn bow.

Roose threw himself to his left as the arrow hit the well wall and veered off in a skyward direction. They'd spotted him, cutting off his chance to move.

Waiting, imagining the Indian with the bow nocking another arrow, he sprang up from his position and put three rapid shots into the stable opening. The bullets slapped into the woodwork, sending up a shower of jagged splinters, but no cries, no blood. Swinging his Spencer again to the cabin he put a further three rounds inside. Spent, he threw the carbine down and drew his Colt Cavalry. Just then more firing opened up. It was close.

Cole sprang out from his cover, standing, legs apart, Winchester lined up as three shots rang out across the wide open area between the rear of the cabin and the stable door.

He saw them. Two warriors, hatchets in hand, quiet as an owl swooping for its prey.

Three more shots thundered into the cabin and Cole responded, pouring steady shots into the charging men. Each bullet struck home, hitting first one man, then the other, full in the chest, throwing them backwards and Cole put two more bullets into each of them, heads erupting in a fine spray of pink mist and white, shattered skull fragments.

A man came out of the stable, drawing a bow and Cole shot him, dropping him like a stone.

The silence descended, eerie, other-worldly and Cole stood and viewed it all, dispassionate, unmoved. He'd fought Comanche for many years. This was nothing new for him. He knew what these warriors were capable of, their ruthless aggression almost legendary. Even in death, they appeared terrifying.

Footsteps clumped around inside the cabin and Cole whirled, going to one knee, his revolver in his hand, the Winchester by his side empty.

The rear door to the cabin remained closed. A voice, one he knew, called from beyond it. 'Cole? It's me. Don't shoot.'

The door eased open and Roose stood there, white as death. 'It's bad, Cole.' He pushed his Colt its holster, angled for a cross-belly draw. 'Very bad.'

Without a word, Cole scooped up the Winchester and pushed past his friend and into the cabin interior.

It took a moment for his eyes to adjust to the change in light.

A large room, where once the family would have sat around the table, eating supper, sharing the laughter, the rigours of the working day. Ordinary conversations. Father, hard-working, wiry, strong. His two sons, gangly, not yet fully filled out. The wife. Plain, but determined. A daughter.

Cole knew all of this. He could see them.

The daughter was outside, next to the well. She must have broken free and run for her life. An arrow in the back.

Is that how it was?

He didn't know about the girl, but he knew about the others.

The wife lay spread-eagled across the table. Naked, her body defiled, her mouth open in a soundless scream, features contorted in pain. After they'd had their fill of her, they'd opened her up like a ripe melon with a heavy-bladed Bowie, straight to the breastbone.

If they had witnessed it, the male members of the family could not have helped her. Both boys were hanging by the feet from the rafters. Naked, the blood running in thick black streams down their bodies to mingle with their matted hair.

Between them, propped against the cold fireplace, the father. They'd wrenched his arms sideways, and lashed his limbs to the mantle to make him appear like a bird of prey, hovering over the dead. They'd hacked off his hands and his feet leaving him to bleed out in a torment of horror, watching what his wife had to endure, unable to help.

'What do we do?'

Cole turned to his friend. Something passed between them. A sadness, but also an acceptance. They had come too late to help these people and that was something that would stay with them forever.

'We bury them,' said Cole dispassionately, 'then we burn this place to the ground.'

Roose cleared his throat, averting his eyes from the horrors around him. 'And Cougan?'

Grunting, Cole went over to their companion. The knife still jutted from his back. It might have been the same knife they'd used on the woman. Cole put one hand flat against Cougan's back and pulled out the broad blade, the flesh making a sucking sound in its desperate attempt to keep the cold metal inside. It came out with a sickening plop and Cole pushed Cougan forward and he toppled, like a great tree, and smacked into the ground, face down.

'After we've buried 'em, we hunt the others down.' Cole turned and stared at his friend. 'Alone. You and me. And when we catch 'em, I'll do to them what they did to these poor folk.'

Roose's eyes came up and he knew that his friend spoke the truth.

CHAPTER NINE

'Things were a lot different then,' said Cole after both men had shared their memories of a quarter of a century before. He stared into the distance, recalling those images, the burning desire for revenge springing to life once more. 'Darn it, *I* was different.'

'And now it's happening again.'

'Hardly the same Sterling. Those who have broken out of the reservation, they'll be nothing like those others.'

'We never did catch up with the leader.'

'He died, I heard it say. Lone Wolf. Someone shot him and threw his body in a sunken hole somewhere down New Mexico way.'

'You believe it?'

Blinking, Cole frowned as he studied his friend. 'What do you mean by that?'

'Just seems strange, that's all. That these others have—'

'Didn't you tell me that it was some young fella who stirred them up, persuaded them to break out?' Roose nodded. 'Well then, it ain't gonna be Lone Wolf. Even if he didn't die with a bullet in his brain-pan, he'd be as old as a coot by now. A shambling wreck. He'd be … good Lord, he'd be nearer ninety years of age.'

"They live a long time I heard it say.'

'Not *that* old, Sterling. And even if he was still alive, I doubt he'd be able to mount a horse and ride. He'd be old and tired and *long* past it.'

'Isn't that what we are, Cole? Past it? Do you think we still have what it takes?' He pulled in a ragged breath and something rattled in his chest, like nails in a rusty bucket. 'I have to tell you, I ain't sure. Maybe we've just outgrown this business, this land. This life.'

Unconsciously, Cole touched the rear of his skull and the heavy bandaging. He gave a chuckle. 'You might be right there, Sterling my old friend. You might be right.'

For a moment the depressed atmosphere bore down on them both like a living thing. It took Cole an effort to shrug it off, but shrug it off he did, and he gathered himself, the lines around his eyes hardening. 'Sterling, let me come with you. If you go out there in this state of mind there's no telling what might—'

'*No Cole*! I told you, you're in no state for riding out on the range,'

'Oh, and you are? I took a bash on the head, Sterling, but you … What you have cuts a darn sight deeper than anything that's happened to me.'

'You're to stay in bed,' it was Maddie, coming through into the bedroom after more than likely listening to their conversation from out on the landing. 'You have to rest. Doctor's orders.'

'Doctor can go—'

'No he can't, Cole,' she said, coming up close. She pressed a hand down on Roose's shoulders. 'I'm none too happy with you going either, Sterling. It's dangerous.'

'No one else is prepared to do it.'

'It makes no sense.' She swept up her skirts and flopped down on the bed. 'So, they broke in and took a few things. None of it is worth dying for.'

'No one is going to die,' said Roose, but nothing in the tone of his voice was convincing anyone.

Maddie sighed. 'You're stubborn, Sterling. Stubborn and stupid.'

'You could just wait for me,' suggested Cole, looking from one to the other. 'That way we could track 'em down together, and if there was any fighting then I could—'

'Trail will be cold by then' said Roose, shaking his head but not daring to hold his friend's eyes. 'It has to be now. If they get away, they'll be back. Yours ain't the only big house stacked full of treasure.'

'Hardly treasure, Sterling.'

'You know what I mean. If we let 'em go every young tearaway from here to Carson City will think they can just ride in here and do whatever they want. I have to find 'em and bring 'em to justice. You know that, Cole.'

Cole grunted, looked at Maddie and, shrugging his shoulders, raised his brows in acquiescence.

She stood arms folded, watching them trot away, leaving Cole's land, taking the well-worn trail north. She watched them until they were mere dots and, even then, she remained where she was, wishing it was all a dream, that she would wake up and find everything was as it should be. Safe. *Normal.*

'He'll be all right.'

Turning she peered down the wide hallway to where Cole himself stood, rock still, a hand pushed out to support himself on the balustrade.

'I wish I could believe you.'

'It's not like it was,' he said, trying his utmost to reassure her. 'All them years ago, when we were out there, the world was different. A savage, untamed land, with dangers around every corner. It ain't like that anymore.'

'I overheard you and what you were saying. There's been a breakout.'

'Yeah, but even that is nothing—'

Maddie held up her hand and cut him off. 'I heard you. Times are different. But I still don't feel I can relax.' One last glance outside, then she swung around and walked straight up to him, taking his face in her hands and kissing him. 'You should be in bed.'

'If you'll come with me.'

Cocking her head, she couldn't help but smile. 'You think you're up to it?'

'Help these old bones up the stairs and I'll show you.'

CHAPTER TEN

They made camp in the bottom of a large dip, where acacia trees gave them adequate shade, and there was grass and water for the horses. Breaking out biscuits and bacon, Notch soon had a fire burning and he mixed the food in a black pan and fried it. The smell of the cooking caused them all to salivate. Notch poured them coffee and they drank with gusto.

'How are you now, Sollo?' asked Pete, leaning back against a well-knotted tree, stretching out his legs with an expression of sheer delight on his face.

'I'm fine." He rolled his damaged shoulder as if to underline his words. "We're a few hours away from Lawrenceville, but it's best if we are rested and fed before we go in. I want us on high alert, boys.'

Notch looked up from stirring the biscuits and fat, 'Why you say that? Expecting trouble?'

Soloman shrugged. He lay flat out on his back, hat over his eyes, arms behind his head. His stomach rumbled loudly. 'Maybe. I don't trust Kestler as far as I can spit.'

'I thought you said you knew him from years back?'

'I do. But that don't make him any less than the snake he is. He's never been totally trustworthy.'

'Then why did you hook up with him?' asked Pete, incredulous.

'Yeah,' said Notch, his voice a low grumble, 'it cost old Peebie his life, didn't it. Was it worth it?'

A heavy silence fell over them, the only sound the sizzling of the fat in the pan. Notch stirred through it half-heartedly. 'That should never have happened. You said the house would be empty.'

'Kestler *told me* it would be empty.'

'And you believed him.'

'I had no reason to doubt him.' Soloman sat up, face red, the anger brewing. 'Understand this, Notch, Peebie's death was not my fault.'

'Never said it was.' Notch shifted position, his mood dark, sombre. 'This is ready. Wish we had some bread.' He scooped out piles of biscuits and bacon onto tin plates and handed them over. Pete took his without ceremony and instantly started cramming huge spoonfuls greedily into his mouth. Soloman took his plate with much more grace, nodding his thanks, and taking his time with his eating.

'I was in the Lucky Dime saloon,' said Soloman, not looking up. 'I'd been spending time there drinking and gambling.

Peebie was doing better than any of us and we had enough money to find us a decent bunkhouse, with grub and a whore or two. On the third morning, Kestler came in. He's a big man, and he seemed to fill the room. Everyone went deathly quiet. He crossed to the bar, ordered whisky for him and his boys, and then he noticed me. Grinning, he came over and put down his glass in front of me. He told me he was pleased he'd bumped into me, that I should drink his drink. I was down to my last few dimes. I guess he knew that. I drank and his smile got wider. He told me he had a deal he'd like to discuss with me, seeing as we went way back.' Soloman played with a clump of congealed biscuit and grease. He studied it for a long time before popping it into his mouth. Licking his lips, he pushed the empty plate away and lay down on his back again. 'We'd first met some years before, taking one of the last great cattle herds up to Wyoming. The railroad followed pretty darned quick after that, put a lot of us out of business. But on this last drive, Kestler and I got friendly. He was making his money selling that beef, and he'd made a lot of it. Said he was going to become sheriff, marshal even, of a frontier town called Lawrenceville. Well, he'd almost done it by becoming a constable there. Now, there he was, telling me his plan.'

Notch put away his plate. 'To break into those big old houses?'

Soloman grunted. 'There was riches in abundance – they was his words. *In abundance.* Apparently, he was bedding one of them cleaners who visited the homes on a regular basis and she told him everything he needed to know. Would you believe it, she even took pictures.'

'Pictures?' Pete laughed, wiping his mouth with the back of his sleeve. 'Shoot, I have seen them. Photographs is what they is called. They is like paintings, only without the colours.'

'That's right,' said Soloman. 'He showed me some taken from the house we broke into. He said he wanted the big vases and the paintings. Said they was the most valuable, but there was also porcelain figures too. From Germany. He wanted them. We was to be extra careful and we—'

'You told us all that,' said Notch, sounding irritated. 'Didn't stop Pete here smashing that big old blue vase though, did it.'

At this, Pete looked up, grease oozing from both the corners of his mouth. 'Notch, that was Peebie.'

'My ass,' spat Soloman. 'I knew it was you.'

'It was that guy coming in the way he did, taking us all by surprise. I thought the house was empty, just like you said it was! Then, him shooting Peebie and all … I just wanted to get out as fast as I could.'

'You said you didn't know who that guy was, didn't you, Sollo?' asked Notch. 'Did Kestler know?'

'Nope. Kestler never gave me no names, just told me to get some boys, break in and get out. Then we was to do the same to two other houses. He drew me a map. Had it all worked out.'

'Reuben Cole. If I'd have known then … I don't think I would have signed up to any of this. Indians call hiom 'He Who Comes'. You know why?'

'No doubt you're gonna tell me.'

'Because he never stops.'

'Never stops what?'

'Stops hunting you until you are dead and buried deep.' He shuddered. 'If I'd have known…'

'You're full of it,' spat Soloman. 'He's dead. I told you.'

'You don't know that – as *I told* you!'

'Pah ...' Soloman rolled over onto his side. 'Kestler wasn't bothered either way. Said he was gonna recruit another gang to do the same further north.'

'Another gang? What is this, Soloman? You never said nothin' about no other gang!'

'Ease up, Notch,' said Soloman, turning over again and re-settling his hat over his eyes. 'We ain't likely to come into contact with them. They're in the north I said.'

'Even so, I don't like the idea of us sharing.'

'Well, whatever happens now,' said Soloman, his voice sounding tired, resigned almost, 'we have a lot of explaining to do. One, we ain't got no vases and two, we never hit the other houses. Kestler ain't gonna be too happy about any of that.'

'But Peebie's death changed everything,' said Pete quietly.

'Sure did,' said Soloman with feeling, 'but I doubt Kestler will see it that way.'

'I swear, I'm truly sorry about that big old vase. You really think he'll be mad?'

'More than mad,' said Soloman. 'He is gonna be pissed.'

CHAPTER ELEVEN

Most mornings Lance Givens would step onto his large, covered porch and gaze upon his land. He'd close his eyes and breathe it all in, giving thanks to God for the many benefits bestowed upon him. It was something of a ritual and if for any reason, he forgot or omitted to send out his prayer to the cosmos, the guilt would gnaw away at him for the rest of the day. In saying that he rarely forgot. A man of strict habits, one might conclude, by viewing him every morning, that he was obsessive. This particular day, without thinking, he pushed through the main door and smiled as the warmth hit him. His eyes were closed. When he opened them, his smile disappeared.

Five riders, in a dark smudged line, were on the distant horizon, moving slowly bit inexorably towards his home.

They were crossing land which was fenced off and had been for well over thirty years. Givens had claimed this land half a lifetime ago, had worked and sweated over it, forging it into the sprawling ranch it now was. To have gained access, these intruders must have broken through the perimeter fence which demarked where the range ended and his ranch began. They'd called him a sod-buster back then. Now they called him 'Mr Givens'. Out here, he was the law. Despite the twentieth century promising wholesale change for the country, this particular plot was locked into days gone by. Givens didn't even possess a telephone.

Perhaps he should.

Swinging around, he stepped back inside. Mooching about in the dining room, laying the table for breakfast, old Shamus looked up and caught something in his master's demeanour. He tensed. 'Trouble, Mr Givens?'

Givens, breaking open the rifle cabinet, took out a Henry repeating carbine and loaded it with the same methodical precision he always used when dealing with firearms. 'Could be.'

Without a word, Shamus went to the same cabinet and pulled out a rifle. No words passed between the two men but when his wife wandered down from the first-floor bedroom, yawning, rubbing her eyes, and spotted them the atmosphere changed. 'What is it?'

Givens worked the Henry's lever. 'Don't know. Riders. They must have broken through the fence and they're heading this way.'

'*Riders*? You mean outlaws?' A strangulated yelp came out of her throat and she clamped a hand over her mouth.

'Go to your room,' he said, voice in control. Confident and strong. How he always was. 'Lock the door and do not open it for anyone.'

'Oh no, Lance, what if they ...'

He forced a smile, but it wasn't entirely convincing. 'Deborah, lock the door. There's a Colt in my dresser. It's loaded. Use it if you have to.'

'Best do what Mr Givens says, mistress.' Shamus eased in the last round in his gun and worked the lever. 'I'll cover you from the first-floor landing.'

Grunting, Givens went to return to the outdoors but checked that his wife was doing as he'd commanded. He saw the trails of her nightdress disappearing up the last few steps of the broad, sweeping staircase and he sighed. He then went outside.

There were only three men now. He blinked a few times. He knew he hadn't imagined their original number and this development concerned him. Thinking the others must have circled to the rear of the house, he checked either side but saw nothing. They were moving fast. Experts.

He dropped to one knee and settled the barrel of the Henry over the porch balustrade. He let them come on. They rode high in the saddle, backs ramrod straight. As they drew closer, he hissed in a breath.

'Indians,' he muttered to himself.

The central figure was young, much younger than his two companions, who were gnarled, grizzled old men, faces tanned and hard like leather, the lines of age deep cracks in their stretched skin. One sported a top hat, out of which sprouted a large black-tipped feather. The other wore his hair long. Both were dressed in old army jackets, the blue dye faded to a dull grey. The younger one wore a white shirt tucked into newly pressed black jeans. A face chiselled out of granite, his features determined. All eyes were bright and alert, darting from side to side, checking for any danger.

At twenty paces they reined in, the horses snorting furiously. This had been a long ride.

'Howdy,' said the young one, putting a forefinger to his forehead. 'Sure is a beautiful morning.'

'You're trespassing,' said Givens, keeping the rifle trained on the young man whom, he suspected, was the leader.

'Oh,' said the man in white, twisting in his saddle, looking to each of his companions in surprise. 'I didn't know that. We thought—'

'This is my land. You must have broken through a fence to gain access.'

Tilting his head, the man in white shook his head, 'No, no, I can assure you, we did not break through anything, sir.'

'Then how did you get through?'

The man chuckled. 'Well, there was a gap, in your fence. We just assumed—'

'There was no gap. I checked the whole perimeter yesterday evening. It's kind of a routine, you see. My men and I.'

This last point was not lost on the others. They grew tense and the older ones grumbled and looked around, agitated. The man in white, however, did not allow his gaze to shift an inch. 'You and your men?' He nodded. 'And where might they be right now?'

'Mister, that is no business of yours. Your *only* business is getting off my property.'

'Like I say, we didn't know this land was—'

'Well, you do now, so scoot!' To give his words greater emphasis, he eased back the hammer. 'Now.'

'That's mighty unfriendly of you, sir. Mighty unfriendly.'

The scream came first, belonging to Deborah, an ear-piercing sound filled with horror, followed by a single gunshot. Shamus' voice crying out, 'Oh no, *please no!*' and a fusillade of small calibre fire.

Givens instinctively stood up and turned to the direction of the shots.

The man in white shot Givens in the back of the head and it was over.

The others whooped, jumped from their horse and tore into the house. Taking his time, the man in white eased himself to the ground, pulled out a load of hessian sacks from behind his saddle and stepped up onto the porch. Givens, at his feet, had his face pressed against the wood planking, eyes wide open, the blood blossoming around his head. The man in white stooped down and plucked the Henry from Givens' dead hands, eased down the hammer and went inside.

After helping himself to some freshly brewed coffee, the young man went to the foot of the stairs. The cries of a woman in distress filtered down to him. He shouted, 'Boys, quit with your recreationals and come down here to help take the stuff.' One of the men from upstairs grunted, another laughed. A single shot put an end to the woman's cries.

They came down, out of breath, one of them stuffing his shirt into his pants, beaming proudly. 'My, she was a beauty!'

'Here,' the man in white threw over a clump of sacks towards the men. 'We have to move fast. It's still early, but he has neighbours and they would have heard the shots. Why didn't you use a knife?'

'The old coot heard us, tried to shoot me.'

'So you put a half dozen bullets into him?'

'I don't know what half a dozen is, Brody, but I shot him to pieces if that is what you mean.'

The man in white, identified as Brody, shrugged and turned away from the big Indian. 'What you did has probably woken up everybody within a hundred square miles and they will soon be heading out this way to investigate.' Shaking his head, he wandered into what he believed could be termed a library, given the number of books lining the walls. He turned and met his companion's hard stare. 'Mr Kestler wants jewellery and silverware, so get to it. The others are already working and you are wasting time – now *move*.'

Ignoring the other's look of outrage, Brody stepped into the library and marvelled at the learning contained in so many leather-bound volumes. Reaching into his pocket he extracted the list he'd been given. Scanning it, he saw no mention of books, which, to his mind, was criminal. On the desk, however, was one item he could readily tick-off. A perfectly made figure of a couple enjoying an afternoon stroll. Two exquisite porcelain figures, the man in a tricorne hat, the lady in a white, flowing dress, the floral motif on the fabric beautifully rendered. Brody shook his head in awe. To have the skill and artistry to produce such a piece of miniature brilliance was something he could only admire.

He savoured the other delights waiting to be discovered in that large, rambling house.

CHAPTER TWELVE

Roose and his men picked up the trail with relative ease. All three were expert trackers, but Nelson Samuels was the most accomplished. It was he who spotted the signs before the others. 'They are heading towards Lawrenceville, that is for sure.'

'It's a half day's ride. We will overtake them if we carry on.'

'The horses need resting.'

'They can rest after we've run those loathsome vermin down.' Roose unconsciously checked the revolver at his waist. 'We have them in our sights and I won't allow them to slip away.'

'You said this was a manhunt, Sterling, not a *death*-hunt.'

'You can ride back if you wish,' said Roose. 'You'll be paid for your time.'

'Ain't no need to say that, Sterling. I'm here to do a job, but I ain't an assassin.'

Roose scoffed, 'Nor me.'

The big man called Cougan stretched out his back. 'You did this with my pappy, didn't you, Sheriff?'

'Sure did.'

'You was hunters of men back then, so I heard tell?'

'This ain't the same thing.'

'Well then.'

'Well then *what?*' Roose rounded on his old friend's son, eyes flashing dangerously. 'They very near killed Reuben, breaking into his home, violating him and his father's memories! And how many other homes have they raised? Answer me that?'

'We don't know about that, Sterling,' said Samuels. 'We don't know anything about these idiots.'

'I know they tried to kill Reuben. If we let 'em go, we'll be sending a signal to every vagabond between here and the Missouri Breaks to come and help themselves to whatever we got!'

'I'm not saying we don't catch 'em, or let 'em go, Sterling. We bring 'em back for trial, that is what I meant.'

'And if they resist?'

Samuels left the question hanging unanswered. He shrugged and turned from Roose's accusing glare.

'Then we kill them,' said Ryan Stone in a flat, unemotional tone.

Roose grunted, flicked the reins and moved on in the direction of Lawrenceville.

When Roose was safely out of earshot, Samuels gave Stone a jab in the arm. 'You up for this, Ryan? Killing these men in cold blood?'

'Shoot Mr Samuels, it's like Mr Roose said – they darn near killed Mr Cole. I say, lay 'em out dead, then I can claim the bounty. Hot dang it, we could be rich.'

'Or end up in hell.'

'Hell don't put food on the table, Mr Samuels.'

'He's got a point,' said Cougan. He steered his horse behind Stone and Roose, setting his gaze towards the horizon.

Samuels remained watching them in silence. It was a long time before he fell in line.

From their vantage point on a towering cliff, Stone had an uninterrupted line of fire as the three robbers idled along across the open prairie.

'You can shoot 'em from this range?'

Stone gave Roose a sideways glance. 'I can shoot 'em, not sure if I could kill 'em though.'

'What about you, Cougan?'

The big black scout pushed back his hat and whistled soundlessly. 'I'd only wing one of 'em at best. The others would spook and ride like they was on fire towards the town.'

'They'd warn everyone that we're coming,' added Stone.

Roose rolled over onto his back and gazed at the sky. 'All right, that being the case, we could wait until they come out of the town. My reckoning is they are going to meet up with someone there, sell their ill-gotten gains, then move on.'

'Who'll do the buying?' asked Samuels, using Roose's field glasses to study the three robbers.

'My guess is Kestler. Nothing goes on in Lawrenceville without his say-so. He has that place wrapped tighter than a Fourth of July firecracker.'

'Kestler is not a man to trifle with, Sterling. You know that.'

'I do, which is why I say we wait for them to come out. There are only two possible exits. East or West. Northern limits are blocked by the mountains. East is back this way, which I do not think they will take due to their fear of being pursued.' He chuckled at this. 'West is their only option, so we go there, set up an ambush, and wait.'

'What about south?' asked Stone, not taking his eyes from his quarry.

'South is a wide open plain with little water and no shade. It has to be West.'

'So we don't shoot 'em now, Mr Roose?'

Smiling, Roose studied both of his eager young sharpshooters. 'No, Ryan. We shoot 'em when they come out.'

'You're insane,' said Samuels, lowering the glasses and shaking his head as if grieving. 'You've already made your mind up to kill them, haven't you.'

'I haven't decided anything. Not yet.'

'Of course you have.' He glared at the others. 'You all have! Dear God, I never thought it would come to this.'

'Me neither, Nelson, but it has. What must be done has to be done.'

'Killing them, like dogs? And without a trial? Is that what we must do?'

'We've been through this, Nelson. You can leave the shooting to me, Cougan, and Ryan if it'll help your conscience.'

'*Help my* ... Sterling, can you hear yourself? Conscience? What you're planning to do here is murder. Nothing more, nothing less.'

'You think them boys would have thought twice about killing Cole? *They* have no conscience, why should I?'

'Because you're a *lawman*, Sterling. Or at least I thought you were! This is not the old days. This is the Twentieth-century. We have laws and men like you are meant to enforce them, not corrupt them.'

'So say-eth the preacher man.'

'You're out of your mind, Sterling.' Samuels threw down the field-glasses and stood up. 'I'll not be part of this.'

'Sit down, Nelson,' said Roose, sitting up, his revolver materialising in his hand. 'I can't have you high-tailing away. Not now. We're too close.'

'What, you gonna shoot me, is that it?' He pointed to the rapidly diminishing figures out on the range far below. 'Your gunshot will alert them, Sterling. You wouldn't want that, now, would you?'

'I said *sit down*, you old bag of wind. If they hear it or not, I ain't bothered. I'll shoot you dead right now if I have a mind to.' He pulled back the hammer determinedly. 'Sit down until they are out of sight, then you can skedaddle.'

'Sheriff,' interjected Cougan quickly, 'you fire that big old police special and those bandidos will bolt for sure.'

Samuels, ignoring this exchange, turned to see Stone staring at him, that same unconcerned look in his eyes. 'Are you just gonna lie there, Ryan and say nothing?'

'Nothing to say, Mr Samuels. I want the bounty, simple as. And if you go back home, then that leaves all the more for me and Cougan here. Mr Roose can't take any, he's the law. I'll be sitting pretty.'

'With blood on your hands!'

Stone shrugged, sighed, and straightened himself up. 'My daddy died last winter, his chest all clogged up with blood and pus. Mama never has got over it. Like an old lady, she is. Mary, my eldest sister, she tries her hardest to cope, but Belinda, our youngest, is not well either. Doc says she has the same as Pa had.' He sniffed, dragging the back of his hand across his nose. 'I gotta do what I can to help my family, Mr Samuels. You go on home if you needs to, but I have an opportunity to make a difference to my loved ones, and I will.'

Looking down, unable to answer any of these points with any conviction, Samuels allowed his shoulders to droop. He turned to Roose and nodded his head. 'Put your gun away, Sterling. I'll go as soon as they are well out of earshot.'

Roose acquiesced and returned his New Model Police to its holster. 'We'll give 'em a half hour then make it over yonder, to the western boundary, and set up amongst the rocks.'

'And what if he tells folk back in town what we is planning on doing?' demanded Cougan, standing at his full, impressive height, agitated, breathing irregular.

From this angle, Roose thought he looked remarkably like his father and, more to the point, appeared just as headstrong and unpredictable. 'He won't,' he said quietly.

'We can't take the risk.'

'What are you saying exactly, Cougan,' spat Samuels. 'I told you, all I want is to go back, take no part in this. I'll not say anything to no one.'

'You will to your wife, we all know it. You cling to her skirts like you is her child. You'll blab to her and she'll tell the whole world and its wife.'

'Hold on there, Cougan,' said Roose dangerously. 'If Nelson says he won't tell, he won't tell.'

'I ain't so sure,' growled the big man and dived for the large Bowie knife at his hip. The great blade flashed. Ryan Stone yelped and scurried backwards on his backside as the big man lunged forward, preparing to swipe Samuels across the throat.

Roose moved before anyone else could even gather their wits. Looping one arm around Cougan's knife hand, he cracked his foot behind the big man's knees. As Cougan buckled and tried to twist himself free, Roose plunged his own knife deep into the big man's back, slicing upwards, the blade cutting through vital organs, piercing the lungs and into the heart. The blood welled over his fist and he held on, pushing ever deeper until he felt the strength leaving Cougan's body. Roose released his hold.

Without a sound, Cougan dropped to the ground, dead.

The others gaped at what had happened, horrified at the swiftness of Cougan's death. Roose stepped back, breathing hard, regarding the corpse with loathing. 'He sure did inherit all of his father's bad habits.'

Ashen-faced, Stone managed a strangulated mumble, 'I ain't ever seen such a thing. What do we do now?'

'Bury him,' said Samuels. He appeared shaken, face drained of colour.

'No. Leave him for the buzzards,' said Roose. 'I'll not waste any more of time on him.'

'Sterling, for the love of decency, you have to—'

'I don't *have* to do a single thing, Nelson, except what I came out here to do. Now leave it all well alone.'

Conversation over, Roose returned to his place, pulling his hat over his eyes and stretching out his long legs.

Stone looked with incredulity towards Samuels, who merely shrugged, slumped down on top of a large boulder and put his head in his hands.

Nobody spoke as, just under an hour later, Roose and Stone eased their horses down from the mountainside and began their crossing of the range to the far western edge of the town of Lawrenceville. Samuels, having said some simple words over the dead Cougan, rode away in the opposite direction without a backward glance.

He made good going, calculating he need only camp out for one night before he returned home to his wife and a good, hearty meal. No doubt she would be full of questions and Samuels already went through a number of scenarios as he set a steady pace along the trail. Cougan's death troubled him. He knew Roose had saved his life, but the enormity of the violence shocked him, left him numb, forcing him to question the Sheriff's sanity. He'd seen a wildness in his old friend's eyes, a loss of control. At the same token, he thanked God for it. Cougan would have murdered him within a blink and would have done so with less conscience than Roose had displayed. A tremor ran through him. He'd rather forget it, as best he could. His only fear now was that his wife would somehow tease it out of him.

Deep in thought, he did not notice the five riders coming out of the heat haze towards him.

By the time he did, it was already too late.

CHAPTER THIRTEEN

Perhaps the most prominent feature of the town was the train station. Two lines, a waiting room, wrought iron canopy and, at that moment, a huge locomotive hissing steam awaiting departure, a man filling the tender with water. The engine throbbed, beating like the heart of some prehistoric beast. Soloman pulled up his horse and breathed in the vapours. 'I don't know what it is, but that smell makes me feel like I'm home.'

Notch sniggered. 'That ain't no home I'd ever like to visit.'

'Notch, I wouldn't invite you anyway.' Soloman sniffed loudly. 'When was the last time you washed?'

'Christmas morning, as always. Don't see no point in washing away my natural oils, Sollo. It's what protects me from diseases.'

'Well you is ripe, my old friend. I reckon when this is done, we book ourselves into a warm, inviting bordello, and ease ourselves into a tin bath full of fancy French perfumes.'

'Hot dang,' cried Pete, tearing off his hat and beating his thigh with it. 'I like the sound of that, by Jiminy! You think Kestler will give us enough dollar to do all that, Sollo?'

'More than enough. He'll be mad about the vase, but the rest will cheer him up.'

'Let's hope so,' said Notch, sounding unconvinced, shooting a derisory sideways glance towards Pete.

They slowly moved away from the bellowing of the locomotive beast and eased their way into Main Street.

Kestler's base of operations did not require a signpost to identify it. Next to the first saloon, they came to a large merchandise store, which bore the legend 'R KESTLER & Co'. Under the shade of an awning, three gunhands leaned against the veranda balustrade, chomping on tobacco or smoking, looking bored. They stiffened as Soloman and the others rode up.

'Howdy,' said Soloman.

The gunhands did not speak.

Soloman shifted his weight in his saddle, the leather creaking. Surveying the street, he noted how quiet it was. What few shops were still open, none appeared to have any customers. It was early evening, the air thick with heat. Maybe that was the reason. He caught Notch's feverish look and tried again. 'I'm looking for Mr Kestler. Is he about?'

'Nope.'

This from the tallest of the three men. He leaned over the balustrade and spat into the dirt next to Soloman's horse. The animal snorted and stamped its foot.

'Do you know where I might find him?'

'Nope.'

He'd tried. Friendly, polite. None of these came easily to Soloman, but he'd done his best. He exchanged another glance with Notch and drew his revolver in one, flowing movement. 'Then do your best to remember, boy, before I put a hole so big in you that fancy new train down at the station could ride right through you.'

The three gunmen stood gawping at Soloman's audacity. The tallest tried his best to laugh, but nothing came out except a strangulated squawk.

Notch and Pete drew their guns.

Soloman grinned. 'I'm waiting.'

'No need for any of that, Soloman.'

Half a dozen pairs of eyes snapped to where a baritone voice boomed. A man dressed in black trousers and waistcoat, watch chain stretched across his ample belly, pulled off his Stetson and mopped his brow with a handkerchief.

'Well how do you do, Mr Kestler,' said Soloman, the relief noticeable in his voice. He dropped his gun back into its holster. 'I was thinking we might have come into the wrong town.'

'Hardly likely, Soloman, seeing as Lawrenceville is the only sizeable settlement in these here parts.'

'I was talking about the reception committee.' He nodded towards the gunmen, who remained nervous, eyes fluttering from Kestler to the others.

'Well, they are raw, Soloman. Unlike yourself. A seasoned campaigner.' He chuckled at his joke. 'Tell your partners to get themselves a drink in the saloon while you and I discuss business in my office.'

'Sounds good to me,' said Pete, holstering his gun.

Notch did not follow suit. He stood, glaring at the gunhands. A friendly tug on the shoulder from his partner eventually made Notch turn and stomp off towards the saloon.

'He's edgy,' noted Kestler, taking Soloman by the elbow and steering him towards the entrance to the large store.

'It's been a difficult few days, Mr Kestler.'

They went inside. Soloman gasped.

A vast space opened up before him, the ceiling so high a double storey house could be placed inside. There were aisles stuffed with every conceivable piece of equipment, from simple hammers and nails to entire ploughs with harness. Every space seemed filled. Sacks full of grain. Great rolls of cloth. Clothing. Boots. Hats. And guns, of course. Lots of guns. Above all, it smelled wholesome, the air rich with sweet, seasoned timber, a smell designed to encouraged a customer to linger, browse and buy.

Soloman whistled through his teeth. 'Dear Lordy, Mr Kestler, this is a mighty fine shop.'

'It's what is known as a supermarket, Soloman. Got the idea after I visited New York city some months back. You like it?'

Soloman shook his head in awe, pirouetting to take everything in. 'It's incredible. But, where is everyone? The town seems almost deserted so how are you gonna make this a success if no one comes in?'

'Ah, Soloman,' Kestler clamped a big hand on Soloman's shoulder. 'It's evening, people have all gone home. Tomorrow it will be bustling again. And of course, now that the railroad is here, soon this entire town will be taking on the look of a city. Already there is building work going on close to the rail station. You might have seen it?'

Soloman frowned, thinking, but he couldn't recall seeing any such building work. Then again, he wasn't particularly looking. 'No, sorry, can't say that I did.'

'Well, not to worry.' Kestler moved through the main aisle towards a broad counter behind which a bespeckled man in a waistcoat and rolled up sleeves was counting money from out of a cash register. He didn't look up as the others approached and Soloman noticed the man's lips moving as he silently counted the cash.

'This is Doc Haynes. He's my chief cashier. A man who knows every inch of this here establishment.' Kestler turned around to face Soloman and leaned back against the counter. 'So, my friend. Did you get it?'

The moment Soloman had dreaded through the entire journey to Lawrenceville was here. He swallowed with some difficulty, spread out his hands, a forced a pathetic smile. 'We had a problem.'

'Ah,' Kestler, nodding, turned askance towards Haynes. 'A problem?'

Did the cashier stop counting, if only for a second? Soloman tensed. The atmosphere was changing. Gone the friendly warmth of the interior, replaced now with a frosty chill. 'Yeah. The house we broke into, the one you told us about ... What you didn't tell us was that the owner was Reuben Cole.'

'Ah. Reuben. He has something of a reputation.'

'It was Notch who recognised him. Said he was an old-time Indian scout for the Army. Hard as they come. A killer.'

'Yes, so I understand.' He drew in a large breath. 'So you killed him?'

'I kicked him to pieces. He shot poor old Peebie right through the head.'

'Yes, but you *killed* him?'

The cashier stopped counting altogether. Soloman waited, trying to steady himself as his heart slammed up into his throat. 'I believe so.'

'Well then,' Kestler clapped his hands together. 'We have no further need to worry do we?' Again, a quick glance towards Haynes who now stood, head down, palms flat on the counter. 'And the items, Sollo? You managed to acquire the items?'

'I have 'em all, tied up with the horses. Except for the vases. The big blue ones.'

An arched eyebrow. A slight draining of colour from the lips. 'Oh?'

'Yeah. Pete, he sort of panicked ...'

'Panicked?'

'Yeah, with Cole coming in and all, shooting Peebie the way he did. Poor Pete sort of got all nervy, knocked into 'em. Smashed 'em.'

'Smashed them?'

Soloman nodded and looked across to Haynes whose own head had come up, eyes filled with a murderous glare. Soloman took an involuntary step backwards. 'Mr Kestler, it was an accident. We got everything else.'

'The painting?'

'Yes, I got that. No problem. Figures too, beautiful things. And serving dishes, as your orders. Solid silver. Soup bowl. Great big thing, with a ladle. All in solid silver. French, I think you said.'

'Yes. Lots of French things. Cole's father was something of a collector.'

'So, from what I'm guessing, you know Cole?'

'I've never met the son, but I have met the father on numerous occasions. Before his untimely death, of course.' As the corners of his mouth turned down, Kestler took on the demeanour of a deeply disappointed man. He sighed long and loud. 'I'm saddened though, Soloman by what you have told me. I thought I could trust you.'

'You *can,* Mr Kestler. You can.'

'Hmmm .... Well, I am not happy. Those vases, they were worth a lot of money. I had customers lined up, all the way from Paris, France.'

Soloman gaped at that. 'Oh, really?'

'Yes, *really.* I have a reputation to maintain, Soloman. I need men on whom I can depend.'

'On whom ...' Soloman's voice trickled away. 'Mr Kestler, this was one mistake. I'm sorry, it won't happen again.'

'Get rid of this Pete fellow.'

It was Haynes, his voice like a slab of ice piercing the heavy air. Soloman turned to him, eyes bulging, his stomach rolling over. 'Get rid of him? What does that mean exactly?'

'It means,' said Kestler, folding his arms, looking smug, 'we can't afford to have idiots working for us, Soloman. Your choice of accomplices was not a good one. You need to vet them much more circumspectly. Understand?'

Soloman didn't. The man was talking in some fancy, made-up way and he could not make head nor tail of his words. He ran a finger under the collar of his grubby, sweat encrusted shirt. 'I, er, don't think I do, Mr Kestler. What does circum, er, circumthingfully mean?'

'You need to take more care in who rides with you,' said Haynes, eyes unblinking, his stare able to freeze bones to the marrow. 'So get rid of him.'

'The other one too. The jumpy one.'

'Notch? But I can't ...' Soloman puffed out his chest. Not used to being spoken to this way, not by anyone, he wasn't about to be railroaded into something he didn't want to do. His hand dropped close to his gun. 'All right, Mr Kestler, we made a few mistakes and I'm sorry. So, if you'll be paying us what we're due, we'll be on our way.'

'On your way?' Kestler chuckled. 'Soloman, you work for me. You can't simply walk away.'

'And I can't simply 'get rid' of my boys. So pay me the money we is owed and that'll be an end to it.'

'No,' said Haynes.

'What did you say?'

'He said 'no', Soloman. I have a business to run and you are part of it. Now, do as you are told or you won't get a single penny.'

'Get rid of them,' said Haynes and added, with deliberate slowness, 'then all of the payment will be yours.'

Running a hand over a face seeping with sweat, Soloman instantly saw the attraction of such a proposition. 'I've known Notch for years,'he spluttered, pressing a trembling hand against his mouth. 'He's my friend.'

The other two men stared. Neither spoke.

A thousand conflicting thoughts roared around inside his head and, with each passing moment, the stress levels increased. Pulling off his bandana, he mopped his brow, puffing his breath through ballooning cheeks. 'I hate you, Kestler. You hear me? You should have told me about Cole and who he was.'

'Just do it,' said Haynes, looking down at the money. 'With less of the dramatics.'

'Just who are you, mister?'

Shaking his head, Haynes returned to counting out the piles of dollar coins and bills.

The conversation was over.

CHAPTER FOURTEEN

Nestling amongst a jumble of jagged rocks, Roose and Stone did their best to stay comfortable, knowing they may well be there for some time. Shade was minimal, a fact not missed by Roose. 'Always had me a wide-brimmed sombrero when I rode with the Army,' he said, readjusting his own headwear, a battered Stetson.

Stone, bareheaded, pulled off his bandana and fashioned a sort of cap which he positioned on top of his skull. 'Stupid. I should have brought something.'

'Too late now,' said Roose, pushing himself up against a large boulder in order to get a good view of the town below. He took up his field glasses and focused in on the main street. Few people were about, one of two wagons moving slowly along, but no sign of the burglars.

'How long do you reckon we should wait?'

'Beats me,' said Roose, lowering the glasses. 'A few hours at least. If my guess is correct, they are down there doing some sort of deal after delivering their stolen goods.'

'Yeah, but who to?'

Another shrug. 'Not sure it matters, but I'm guessing Kestler.'

'Yes, the one you mentioned. He runs the town, so you said.'

'He does, but I ain't ever heard of him doing anything illegal.'

'Always a first time.'

Roose looked at his young partner and chuckled. 'That there is. You learn fast, son. It is to the advantage of a lawman to get inside the head of those he pursues and that is what you is doing.'

'Is that what you did when you hunted Comanch? Get inside their heads?'

Roose turned away. 'Comanch is different. They don't think like White folks. That's what makes 'em so dangerous.' His eyes grew cloudy as he looked back to a time steeped in brutality and death. 'They is a proud and noble people, but if you cross them they will not rest until you are under their knife. They give no quarter and they expect none.'

Finally satisfied with his protective cap, Stone took the chance to sit up and peer down to the township of Lawrenceville. 'They must have been dangerous times back then.'

'Times is always dangerous, son, if you do not keep your wits about you,' he patted the New Model Police in its holster, 'and always have your best friend forever close.'

Nodding in agreement, Stone settled himself back down amongst the rocks. He closed his eyes.

'If you can sleep, do so,' said Roose. 'I'll wake you if anything happens.'

As he did not possess a timepiece of any description, Roose had to rely on his age-old abilities to calculate the hour by the passage of the sun. Satisfied they had waited for well over three hours and with the evening hurrying on, Roose roused his young companion with a sharp dig in the ribs with his boot. Stone cried out, arms flailing, and sat up, disorientated. 'What? What is it?'

'It's late and there's no sign of anyone. I've been watching and watching but there ain't nothing.'

Stretching out his limbs, Stone climbed uncertainly to his feet. 'It's almost evening. You should have woken me earlier, Mr Roose.'

'The day's moving on, yes, but you were sleeping like a baby.' He gave Lawrenceville one last look through the field-glasses then dropped them back into their leather case. 'I'm going down there.'

'What, into the town?'

Roose grunted before he checked his revolver. 'We'll go in nice and slow, but from the other side. It's an easier approach, given that we won't need to take our horses on such a treacherous downward route. Take a look.'

Stone craned his neck to take in the twisted, rutted path that snaked down towards the town. Given its steep angle of descent, it did indeed appear perilous.

They moved off, Roose in the lead. Having covered almost three-quarters of the distance between their hilltop lookout and the eastern entrance to the town, Roose brought his horse up to a jerking halt, right hand raised. 'Dismount,' he said, voice reverting to the tone of authority that served him so well in his army days. Without waiting for his younger companion, he dropped from the saddle and scurried over to a clump of sage and got down on his knees. Silently, Stone followed, something which didn't go unnoticed. 'Good,' acknowledged Roose and brought up his field glasses. He trained them towards the open prairie and sucked in air through his teeth. 'Shoot,' he said and passed the binoculars to Stone.

There were riders, moving at a leisurely pace, the man at the lead of the group distinctive in a blazing white shirt. Alongside him, the horse tied to his own, the rider manacled, stripped to the waist, was Nelson Samuels.

'Oh no, they captured Mr Samuels.'

Roose took back the glasses and looked again. 'All right, at least he's alive. They must be taking him into town, maybe to question him.'

'Question him? About what?'

'Who he is, why he's out here all alone, why he's packing a rifle that can take your eye out at a thousand yards.' He pushed the binoculars into their leather case and closed the lid. 'Whatever they ask, they will get their answers and Nelson will tell them everything they want to know.'

'You can't know that Mr Roose.'

'By the look of that band, son, I'd say it's pretty clear who they are – the bunch of Comanch that recently broke out of the reservation.'

'But why are they coming here?'

'Same reason those ones who broke into Cole's place came here – to get paid.'

'By Kestler?'

Grunting, Roose went back to his horse. 'Son, I'm going down there. Maybe I can find out what's going on, negotiate with 'em.'

'Mr Roose,' said Stone, voice verging on breaking, frantic with concern. 'If what you suspect is true, those men won't want to negotiate with you about anything.'

'Yes, they will because you is going back to telegraph for help. There is a detachment of U.S. cavalry at Carson City. You send word there to a man called Willets. Captain Willets. I served with his uncle, Sean Willets, so if you mention my name he'll respond more quickly.' He turned, eyes burning. 'You tell him to send a troop to Lawrenceville, you hear me. And you tell 'em to get here *fast*.'

'Maybe I should go straight to Mr Cole. He'll know what to do.'

'Cole is convalescing. Don't trouble him with any of this.'

'But Mr Cole is—'

Without warning, Roose's hand shot out and seized the young man by his shirt front. 'You do as you are damn well told, you hear me!'

Stone, rigid with surprise and fear, eyes bulging, sweat breaking out on his brow, rapidly nodded his head.

Roose let him go and swung up into his saddle. 'I didn't mean to scare you, son, but this is something I must do on my own. Now get out of here, keep your head down, and don't stop for anyone. You understand me?'

'Yes sir,' said Stone, bringing his heels together, right hand springing against his head in as close an imitation to a salute as he could make.

Wheeling his horse away, Roose cantered off, back ramrod straight, determination evident in every part of his body.

Stone watched and wondered if life was ever going to be the same again.

CHAPTER FIFTEEN

It was Pete who first reacted when Soloman came through the batwing doors. He nudged Notch who sat absently dealing out cards for a game of Patience. 'He's back,' he said.

Notch gave Soloman a frown as his friend approached their table. 'Well? What did he say?'

'He ain't happy,' said Soloman, dragging a chair from under an adjacent table and sitting down next to Notch. 'Not happy at all.'

'But did he pay us?'

'Not yet. He wants to check through what we managed to get.'

Laying down his undealt cards, Notch allowed his eyes to roam away from Soloman to settle on the gunhands propping up the bar. 'He sure does seem to have quite a few men, don't he? Maybe he's expecting trouble of some kind. I don't like this, don't like it at all. You think he's set on double-crossing us?'

Grunting, Soloman folded his arms. 'We need to talk. There are some complications.'

'Oh? Such as?'

'Such as we need to go out back and talk.' He glanced over at the bar. 'Nothing within earshot.'

'You got a plan?' asked Pete, leaning forward. His lean, hungry looking face was streaked with dirt and sweat. Soloman sniffed and turned away. 'Yeah, I know I stink,' Pete sulked, picking up on Soloman's reaction. 'Thought we was getting a bath?'

'Later. We talk first.' Soloman stood up and readjusted his sagging trousers.

'Let's make it quick,' said Notch, 'because I too need a bath.'

Crossing over to the bar, Soloman asked the barkeeper if there was a rear entry. Puzzled, the man somewhat reluctantly pointed to a door at the foot of the large curving staircase that led to upstairs rooms. The landing, which led to a series of closed rooms, was supported by solid wooden posts with empty tables between. 'Not the most popular of places this, is it,' commented Soloman. The barkeeper ignored him. Giving his thanks, Soloman caught the gunhands' scowls and winked. Gesturing for his companions to follow, he went through the door.

The sun was swiftly descending by now and already the air was filled with the sound of insects as Soloman pushed through the door and stepped into a high-walled courtyard, filled with oak barrels and crates. He watched as Notch and Pete joined him.

'Close the door,' he said.

It was Pete who did so, turning his back for one moment.

The only moment Soloman needed.

He drew the heavy bladed Bowie knife from its scabbard positioned in the small of his back and plunged it straight into Notch's midriff, slicing upwards to the breastbone. Notch, so startled he did not have time to yell out, stood there, looking down at the blade in disbelief. Stepping `past him, Soloman smacked Pete across the jaw with his revolver, smashing him back against the door. Grunting, mouth cracked open and full of splintered teeth and frothing blood, Pete did his best to remain on his feet, clawing for his gun. Soloman's knee rammed up into his groin and Pete buckled and crumpled, squealing.

On his knees now, trying to dislodge the knife, Notch bleated like a goat. Soloman came up to his victim's front, put a hand around the knife handle and a boot against Notch's chest and hauled backwards with all his strength. The blade came out, making a sickening squelching, sucking sound as it popped free.

'Why,' hissed Notch before Soloman put the blade into his throat and finished him.

Writhing on the ground, it was clear Pete would not be going anywhere, so Soloman took his time, straddled him, and stabbed his former companion repeatedly until he moved no more.

Soloman stood up, hands and shirt front splattered with blood. He was shaking, but at least it was done. He'd honoured his part of the deal, now Kestler must honour his.

But first, he needed that bath.

. . .

'What is it now?'

Hearing the approaching clump of cowboy boots on the boardwalk, Kestler, sitting at his dinner table and about to tuck into a plate of steak and eggs, lowered his head in despair.

'Boss,' called one of his men, coming into the room at a run.

'What do you want, Bart? Can't it wait?'

'Not really,' said Bart Owens, coming up to the table. 'I'm sorry, Mr Kestler. Truly.'

'Just get on with it.'

'It's them Indians you hired.' Kestler looked up, interest piqued. 'They is outside, horses laden down with sacks and all.'

'Well, that's good news. 'bout time I had some *good* news.'

'They got someone with 'em. They said you'd be interested.'

'Who is it?'

'Beats me.' He forced a smile. 'I, er, think they'd like you to go have a look-see, boss.'

Throwing his chair back with such great force that it toppled over and crashed to the floor, Kestler stood up. 'Looks like I'd better get straight to it, then.'

'Boss, I'm sorry, if I'd have—'

'Ah, shut up, Bart!'

Kestler pushed past him, fuming.

Outside, the steely grey evening lent an eerie aspect to the riders waiting in the street. Drained of all colour, it was difficult to make out their features. Kestler, however, recognised their leader almost immediately, his white shirt acting like a form of spotlight, drawing his attention. Beside him was a stranger, unlike the other riders, head bowed, hands lashed behind his back, naked except for a piece of flimsy, filthy material hiding his nether regions. He was a bloody mess.

'Evening Mr Kestler.'

'Evening Brody.' Kestler said, acknowledging the rider in the white shirt. He stepped down into the street, went up to Brody's horse, and stroked its nose. He nodded towards the naked stranger, who appeared semi-conscious. 'Who's this?'

'Well,' Brody brought up his left leg and crossed it over his right, 'we found him out on the range as we were coming here. Something about him …' Tutting, he shook his head. 'Had himself a big rifle. Looked tasty, When I asked him about it, he became all cagey, like. Wouldn't answer, said he had to get back home to Freedom.'

'Freedom? That's the town where I sent you to break into those houses.'

'Exactly, Mr Kestler. So, we decided to rough him up a little so he'd tell us exactly who he is and what he's doing such a long way from home.'

Kestler stepped closer to the stranger and looked him over. Not a young man, his lily-white body was nevertheless well-muscled, as if he took good care of himself. 'What's his name?'

'Calls himself Nelson Samuels. Of course, he didn't give that up straight away.' Brody cackled. 'We had to tease it out of him.' This comment brought great amusement to the other riders.

'I don't know that name.'

'He then told us he was part of a team on the trail of the men who broke into Reuben Cole's house and stole some of his best wares.'

'That would be Soloman's attempt to do my bidding.' Kestler wandered across to one of the other riders and felt through one of the many sacks dangling over the horse's rump. 'Unlike yourself, Soloman's venture was something of a disaster,' said Kestler, in a satisfied tone. Brody was the 'real deal'. A man who did as he was told, who got results. 'Did he tell you where the other pursuers are?'

'He told us they were close, coming into town, hot on the gang's trail. That the leader, a man called Roose, was determined to kill the one known as Soloman. Maybe even you, Mr Kestler.'

At this, Bart Owens cleared his throat, 'Maybe we should prepare a welcoming committee?'

Nodding, Kestler clapped his hands together. 'All right, take this one,' he jabbed his fingers towards Samuels, 'and put him in one of the stables over at the livery. When his friend Roose comes along, we'll reintroduce them.'

'After we have some fun?' asked one of the other riders, a big man, aged, grizzled, a deep scar running down the left side of his face.

'Fun?' Kestler arched an eyebrow towards Owens. 'Just get this one tied up in the livery. We'll worry about Roose when he appears.'

'I think we could ambush Roose before he gets into town,' said Brody. 'If he is determined to kill both Soloman and you, it might be best to do as your man here says and stop him before he gets too close.'

'Especially if he has one of those Sharps rifles,' added the scarface. 'With that, he could shoot you from a distance.'

'Yes, all right,' said Kestler, twisting his mouth into something akin to a smile. 'Meanwhile, I want you to take all of the goods you got into my mercantile store. Doc Haynes will sort through it, then pay you.'

From across the street, half hidden behind the side wall of a carpenter's shop, Soloman watched the Indians half dragging a naked man into the livery stables. Others unloaded their horse, together with the bags draped over Soloman's horses. He debated whether or not to stride over and shoot them down dead, but common sense proved the victor on this occasion. There were too many of them. And, unlike Pete and Notch, these men seemed tough and so would prove a much more dangerous proposition. He'd need to bide his time, but with the bags of loot and stolen goods now inside the mercantile store, hopes of recouping any money for his efforts seemed increasingly like nothing more than a distant dream.

Unfortunately, as he stood mulling over his dwindling options, Soloman's nature asserted itself. He knew he would be going up against men who were as violent as he, but the draw of the money was a powerful one, urging him forward, demanding he do his utmost to gain what was his by right.

The men reappeared from the stable, not much more than dark shadows now as night continued to conquer the light. They were laughing with one another as they made their way to the mercantile store. Checking his revolver, Soloman decided to act quickly. He would interrogate the man in the stable first, find out what was going on, then charge into the store, killing whoever got in his way. The time for niceties was over. The time for action was here.

A stream of light pierced the darkness and Soloman's attention was drawn to the mercantile store entrance. The men entered, the glow from inside friendly and inviting. He chuckled. He would be the uninvited guest, the unexpected one. But not one that any person inside would welcome. He went to emerge from his hiding place, but before he could cut across the street a movement over to his right forced him to quickly return to behind the wall.

A figure appeared out of the shadows and scurried towards the stable. As he squinted, trying to focus in on who it might be, he caught the sound of a dress swishing across the ground.

It was a woman.

CHAPTER SIXTEEN

She'd been walking for some time, deciding against taking her colt up into the hills, which is what she normally did. This particular evening, with the stars so bright and the air so mild, she wanted to stroll through the streets of what used to be a friendly, convivial town. Since Kestler and his boys rode in all those months ago, beat up poor old Stefan Moss, the sheriff, and sent him packing, everything had changed. Lawrenceville was now a miserable place to live. People moved away whenever they could, but recently Kestler's men kept a much tighter rein on people's movements. Things took a turn for the worse on the fateful night Kestler took a shine to her, approached her in the street, and invited her for dinner.

'I'm a married woman,' she said, not that that was her only reason for rejecting his advances. Kestler disgusted her. And not only his reputation. He was overweight, a whisky drinker, an arrogant, spiteful man, well used to getting his own way.

'You're a sweet young thing,' he'd said to her, swaying as he spoke, much the worse for drink. He stroked her cheek. She flinched. 'Aw, don't be like that,' he'd said, feigning being hurt. 'You entertain me and I'll reward you handsomely. What's your name, my little sweety.'

'I'm not your anything.' He blew a raspberry and she looked away as a rush of whisky breath wafted over her. 'It's Mrs Childer if you must know.'

He chuckled, 'First name is what I meant.' He made a grab for her, which she easily dodged. He almost fell on his face as he lost balance.

'My, you're a feisty one,' he said, leaning against the wall of the saloon out of which he'd emerged to accost her. 'I like that.'

She stepped away but had only managed two steps when he was at her again, pulling her around by the arm to face her. 'Mrs Childer, I am an honourable man,' he was wagging his finger in front of her face, 'Please, do me the service of accepting my invitation to dinner.'

'No.'

Again she went to turn away and again he turned her by the arm. 'I won't ask so politely again.'

'Mr Kestler, I am sure you are well used to getting whatever it is you set your heart on, but I have no intention of accepting your invitation, or anything else for that matter.'

'How does five hundred dollars sound?'

She stopped. Everything stopped, except her mouth which hanged open as if yanked downwards by an invisible cord.

Kestler laughed. 'That's got your attention, eh?' He moved in close, snaking his arm around her waist. 'I mean it. Come to dinner and I'll give you five hundred dollars. It's a present, Mrs Childer, not a payment if you get my meaning.'

She went to strike him, but it was a half-hearted effort and, despite him being drunk, he managed to block her blow and gripped her wrist. 'I'm not a whore,' she hissed.

'I never thought you were. But I'm guessing five hundred will ease your situation.'

Ease her situation five hundred dollars undoubtedly would, but how did he know that? Back home, with his face forever in his hands, her husband Stacey would nightly hurl out abuse at God, the world, and every person in it, blaming everybody but himself for the failure of his bean crop. He'd put everything they had in purchasing the seedlings. Planted them, cared for them, watched them day and night. They'd shrivelled and died. People in town had warned him about the bad choice of land, how irrigation was virtually impossible, how the previous owners of their homestead had experienced similar calamities, first with wheat, then corn. Nothing grew out there, everyone said. Stacey ignored them, dug in the fertiliser, worked in whatever goodness he could. All for nothing. Now those beans, together with all their savings, lay dying in the dust.

So five hundred dollars could give them a new start. A chance to leave, start over in a more forgiving place. She'd always had ambitions to open a store dealing in dry goods. Such a payment could set her up, help purchase enough stock and pay for the initial rental.

Kestler, aware of her hesitation, like the predatory animal he was, swooped. 'I'll make it seven hundred and fifty. Come dine with me this evening. Seven o'clock shall we say?'

She took a deep breath. Seven hundred and fifty dollars. She couldn't earn that in a year working for doctor O'Henry as his receptionist. Not even two years. She'd be a fool to reject this offer if it was only dinner. She suspected, however, for that amount, Kestler would demand a lot more. The thought turned her stomach.

'Listen,' he said, as if reading her mind, 'it'll just be dinner. If anything develops, then that will be just fine. But, I'm not looking for you to do anything you would not want to.'

'Just dinner?'

He nodded, grinning. 'I'll even pay you up front.' He turned away slightly, teetering for a moment before he gathered his strength and pulled out a wallet from inside his coat. He extracted a roll of dollar bills. She gaped, never having seen such a pile of money before. Without a word, he peeled off several bills and pressed them into one of her hands. 'That's two hundred. Come tonight, I'll give you the balance. My housekeeper is a wonderful cook.'

Gazing at the money in her hand she had a sudden urge to pinch herself. This couldn't be happening. *Two hundred dollars? Just like that?*

'If you decide not to come,' he said, beginning to move away uncertainly on legs which barely seemed capable of keeping him upright, 'I quite understand. But keep the money.' He reached the saloon steps, held onto one of the posts adjacent to them and slumped down on his backside. 'Come to the store. We'll take a buggy out to my place.' He looked up, bleary-eyed. 'And your name, Mrs Childer. What's your name?'

'It's Amy,' she said as she moved away, light-headed, unsure of the propriety of her decision, but knowing that the lure of so much money was too powerful to refuse.

After her evening with him, however, her thoughts were to change.

Stacey was drunk when she arrived home after her so-called 'dinner date'. He did not notice her cut lip, dishevelled bodice. As she stumbled around in the dark, found the washing basin and threw water over her face, his snoring grew louder and she thanked God that he could not hear.

It had all happened so unexpectedly.

Kestler, standing outside the mercantile store, well dressed in a neatly pressed morning suit, gold watch chain stretched over his ample stomach, greeted her with a warm, open smile. The heavy smell of cologne invaded her nostrils as she stepped up close. A darn sight more acceptable than whisky fumes, she told herself. He took her hand, kissed it in the finest manner, opened the door and motioned her inside.

The inside of the store was vast, lit by numerous gas lamps which gave off a thick, oily smell and cast weird, contorted shadows across the walls and ceiling. Everywhere she looked she could pick out the various types of products for sale, from claw hammers to wash basins and everything in between. 'You run a successful business, Mr Kestler.'

'I do indeed,' he said, slipping his arm around her and guiding her to the counter. He lifted up the hatch and led the way through a door in the rear to reveal a small room, candles giving off an inviting glow. A table was laid for two, but there was no food or plates, only waiting cutlery and napkins. 'I have decided it best to dine here, rather than at my home. My housekeeper will arrive later with our dinner.'

Smiling she waited until he pulled out a chair for her. He was certainly a gentleman, as unlike Stacey as she could imagine. Stacey was roughly hewn, his hands large, calloused, his body tight with muscle from the many hours he laboured in the fields. But his brains were addled, the drink rendering him little more than a mulling fool nowadays. Kestler, although clearly a drinker, seemed far more in control of himself. Successful and sophisticated.

'You are so very attractive, Amy,' he said, producing a bottle of wine from a cabinet in the corner. He poured a generous measure into a delicately cut glass. She smiled, a little coy, sweeping away a lock of hair, and raised the glass as he clinked his own against hers. She drank, the wine tasting crisp, sweet and unlike anything she had ever sampled before. 'I'm surprised your husband let you out so late, to meet a strange man.'

'Stacey was asleep, as usual.'

'Ah yes. He spends a good deal of his time asleep, so I hear.'

About to take another sip, she paused, eyes studying him through hooded lids. Slowly, she lowered the glass. 'What else have you heard, Mr Kestler?'

'That you're lonely. Unhappy. A husband who pays you no attention does not lead to a satisfactory relationship.'

'Is that right?' She sat back in her chair, the heat rising to her jawline. 'You've been asking about me, is that it?'

'I'm *interested* in you, Amy. As soon as I first saw you something happened to me,' he punched his chest, 'in here, in my heart.'

'Well, that's all very complimentary, Mr Kestler, but I don't really think I can—'

Without warning, he reached across the table for her, seizing both her wrists in his hands. Taken completely by surprise, she gave a startled shriek. He pulled her towards him. 'Amy, I'm only asking for you to give me a chance. Please, We can have several evenings such as this, develop our friendship.'

She struggled in his grip. 'Mr Kestler, you're hurting me.'

But she saw then there was something in his eyes. A change, all of his self-control disappearing with each passing moment. 'You don't understand.'

'I understand perfectly,' she said, voice breaking as she tried to pull herself free from his hold. But he was surprisingly strong and then, unbelievably, he was leaning across the table to plant a wet kiss on her mouth. Squirming, she managed to turn her head so that his lips smacked against her cheek. 'I can look after you,' he cried, his face so very close now, the broken veins on his bulbous nose appearing large at this distance. 'Please, just give me the chance to show you. I can't resist you, Amy. I can't.'

Summoning all her strength, she at last managed to tears herself free and jumped to her feet. Crying out, she made to run, but he was there, moving faster than she could ever imagine, catching her around the waist, turning her, kissing her again, this time with success.

He was moaning and she could feel his hardening manhood pressing against her. Ripping her lips free, she slapped him hard across the face. Gasping, he recoiled, clutching at his rapidly reddening cheek. 'You bitch,' he said.

She hit him again, rocking him back against the table. Turning she made a grab for the door handle. He caught her, strong hands gripping her arm, bringing her round to face him. This time it was his turn to strike, a forceful back-handed blow across her mouth which rattled her teeth. Her legs buckled under her, strength seeping from her muscles, and another back-handed slap from the opposite direction sent her to the floor.

Head spinning, she had only the vaguest notion of where she was or what was happening. Material ripped, hot lips pressed against an exposed nipple. Hands clawed at her dress, her undergarments. Through a swirling mist, she saw him groping for his own pants, the belt pulling away, the flies opening.

From somewhere she trawled up enough strength to swing her booted foot into his groin. He screamed, staggered backwards and hit the table again. Curled up in a ball, hands clamped over his crotch, eyes squeezed tight shut, tears sprouting, he wailed like a baby.

Rolling over onto her knees, she pressed the back of her hand against her mouth, felt the blood, cursed herself for being so stupid. Using the door handle for support, she hauled herself to her feet and looked at him writhing on the ground. 'I'll kill you if you ever come near me again,' she said and went out into the store.

Moving like a drunkard, she waltzed through the aisles, bashing into the occasional display, sending stacks of pots, pans, culinary utensils and crockery crashing to the floor. Unconcerned, she continued to the main door and stepped out into the night. The cold, night air hit her almost as hard as Kestler's blows, but it revitalised her, cleared her head. She managed to get to her buggy and, without a single pause, flicked the reins over the colt's back and soon she was riding away into the night, leaving Kestler hurt, pride broken, alone in his room, to recover.

And now, here she was. She'd watched them take the semi-naked stranger into the stable. Waiting, she now moved closer. Since that night, Kestler had attempted no further advances, but she continued to seethe about the money. He owed her and, from her standpoint, she had every right to it. Perhaps this was a way to make some form of redress. So she crept up to the stable door and eased it open.

CHAPTER SEVENTEEN

The shadows were long as Roose came into town, walking his horse slowly down the middle of the main street. Shops and stores on either side were now closed for business, the last few owners sweeping away the dust from their porch entrances. One or two looked up as he passed by, their faces framed by the flickering lights from the interior of their businesses. Roose, eyes straight ahead, made for the only building which appeared open. The saloon. A chipped and faded sign across the front bore the name 'Lucky Nights' which he thought somewhat amusing, given the virtual absence of customers.

A solitary man sat on a rocking chair adjacent to the batwing doors. He busily filled a bone pipe as Roose dismounted, tied up his horse, dusted off his jacket and took the steps to the boardwalk. The man looked up. 'Evening,' he said in a lazy drawl, settled the pipe stem between his teeth, struck a long match and set it to the filled bowl.

Roose tipped his hat. 'I'm looking for a Mr Kestler.'

The man paused in concentrating on lighting his pipe. His face clouded over. 'And why might that be, mister?'

'Is he inside?' Roose went to take a step forward.

'I asked you a question, boy.'

This remark amused Roose as he was considerably older than the pipe-smoker. 'All I wanna do is talk to him.'

'Well, you can wait here while I go and have a look-see.'

'Kinda touchy, ain't you?'

'Just doin' my job, boy,' said the man, discarding his pipe and standing up.

Roose noted the brace of Army Colts in the man's waistband. 'And what job might that be?' Without waiting for a reply, he pulled back his coat to reveal the badge pinned to the left lapel of his waistcoat. 'This here is mine.'

Pursing his lips, the pipe-smoker turned and dipped through the doors without another word.

Roose waited. There was little noise emanating from inside, perhaps because it was early, or perhaps because few people frequented this establishment. The entire town had a sadness about it, even the buildings appearing sullen, uninteresting. It stank with the air of decay and Roose doubted it would remain inhabited for much longer and would fade away, like so many other frontier towns through the West. As the big cities of San Francisco and Los Angeles grew, so the numerous towns which sprang up along the newly laid railroad lines to house the many labourers died. Ghost towns they called them. As he waited, Roose wondered how many souls had come to such places in search of dreams and new beginnings only to have those aspirations crushed, trampled into the dust.

He gave a jump as the double doors sprang open. The pipe-smoker stood in the doorway, but he was no longer alone. A large man filled most of Roose's view together with several other men, mean-looking, all of them toting tied down guns, hate-filled bearing down on the sheriff.

Maintaining his calmness, Roose inclined his head slightly. 'Mr Kestler, I assume?'

'That's right,' said the big man, 'but you have me at a disadvantage, sir. Who may you be?' He wore an embroidered shirt, sleeves rolled up, a glistening film of sweat covering his furrowed brow. Grease around his mouth declared he'd only just finished eating.

'Name's Roose. Sterling Roose. I'm sheriff of Freedom, a small town some fifty miles or so east from here, on the trail of several varmints that broke into and stole some valuable artefacts from my friend's home. Reuben Cole is my friend's name. Perhaps you've heard of him?'

Kestler gave the impression of thinking for a moment. Poking the tip of his tongue between his lips, he savoured the remnants of his dinner before shaking his head slightly. 'Can't say I have.'

'Well,' Roose looked around him, noticing two further men appearing from the side of the saloon. They must have come from the rear entrance. Both sported Winchesters, 'Thing is, Mr Kestler, I followed the trail of those men straight to this town.'

'Oh, you did?'

'Yes, I did. Perhaps you could let me have a look around, discover any signs that they might still be here.'

'They ain't.'

'Oh.' The men behind him were drawing closer. 'And how would you know that, Mr Kestler?'

'Because I know everything in my town.' As if given some unspoken command, the others eased past their boss, fanning out on either side of him. Four to the front, two to the rear. Roose knew the odds were stacked against him.

'Yes, of course, you do. So perhaps you could tell me which way they headed ... If they have left town, that is?'

The unmistakable sound of Winchester levers engaging accompanied Kestler's broad smile. Roose allowed his shoulders to droop. There was little he could do unless he made a fight of it with his certain death the inevitable outcome. He slowly put up his hands. A tall gangly gunfighter stepped up to him and pulled out Roose's handgun.

'You on your own?' asked Kestler as the others moved up to Roose and took him by the arms.

'I am.'

'A manhunt with only one in the party? I don't think so. We already have one of your boys over in the barn.' Roose's eyes widened despite his best efforts to conceal his surprise. 'So, I reckon there's more of you.'

'Well, there ain't.'

The first fist erupted into Roose's guts with the force of a mule's kick, doubling him up. He gasped and retched as he hung in the firm grip of the men holding him. 'You'd be wise to tell us everything you know,' said Kestler before giving the gangly one a nod. Grinning, the tall gunfighter hit Roose in the midriff again with his left, then followed it up with a right cross to the jaw that almost lifted Roose off his feet.

Hanging in the men's arms, Roose managed to bring his head up as Kestler stepped closer. 'How many more of you are there?' All he received was a slight shake of the head. Kestler nodded again to the tall, gangly one, 'Rough him up a little more, Bart.' Requiring no further encouragement, Bart Owens pulled back his fist in preparedness for another punch. Before he could deliver the blow, a voice came out of the darkness.

'Leave him to me, Mr Kestler.'

Brody emerged from the darkness, his white shirt casting him in its own particular aura. Beside him were his men, gnarled, aged native Indians, eyes feverish, bodies tense with expectation.

'We're more than capable,' said Owens, unable to keep the anger out of his voice.

'You'll kill him before he speaks,' said Brody.

'I have known men like this one,' said the scarface, studying Roose intensely. 'They never speak unless the right pressure is applied.'

'And you can give that pressure?' asked Kestler.

'I can.'

'Then do it. I don't like the idea of more of these scum wandering around my town.'

Reluctantly Owens stepped away as the Indians took hold of Roose and dragged him into the night.

'We will take him just outside of town,' said Brody, then added with a grin, 'so nobody can hear his screams.'

CHAPTER EIGHTEEN

From out of the far distance, Samuels heard something. It might have been the rustling of rats but something told him differently. He eased himself up to a sitting position, grunting with the pain lancing through his ribs. They'd beaten him expertly, pummeling his ribs and guts before stripping him, pressing the broad-bladed knife over his manhood. 'It will only take a second,' said the one in white, that sadistic grin set like a permanent feature on his face. Using the blunt edge, he lifted up Samuels' member. 'A quick flick of this blade ...' He chuckled. 'It'll hurt, my friend. It will hurt a lot. So tell me all that you know.'

Within a few minutes, Samuels revealed everything. That there were two more men in his party, that he wanted no more of it, that Roose's plan was to kill them all, especially the ones known as Soloman and Kestler.

He left nothing out, even telling the man in white it was Reuben Cole's house that had been burgled and that Cole, as soon as he had recovered from his attack, would be out on the range himself, hunting them all down. If anything happened to Roose, Cole's revenge would be terrible.

'Sounds like quite a man,' said the man in white, returning his knife to its scabbard at his waist.

'He is. He's an Indian fighter from the old days.'

The man in white looked at his companions. 'You heard of him?'

Two of them nodded, a tall, heavy set man with a deep scar running down the side of his face, spoke in low, concerned tones, 'He is well known to us. From the old days. He tracked our fathers, put many of them in the ground. My people call him 'He Who Comes'. Nothing can stop him, Brody.'

'Is that right.' Brody stood up. 'Kestler needs to hear this. We'll take this one into town.'

And so they did and now, sitting in the darkness of the stable, the smell of wet hay thick in his nostrils, Samuels held his breath, straining to hear the scurry of the rats again. The scurry when it came, however, was not that of a rat.

A figure squatted down in front of him.

'I watched them bring you in.'

A woman, sounding scared. He couldn't make out her features in the dark, but something told him she was kind. Young. A blade flashed and she was cutting through the cords binding his wrists. 'We're getting out of here,' she said in a whisper. 'I don't know who you are or what you're doing here, but any enemy of Kestler's is a friend of mine.'

Rubbing his wrists, Samuels climbed to his feet. She helped him. Acutely aware of his nakedness, he leaned away. 'I can't walk around like this.'

'I have blankets in my buggy. My home is out of town and once we're there, we can work out what to do.'

'What to do? There's nothing we can do.'

'Oh yes there is,' she said through gritted teeth. 'We can kill him.'

Amy Childer helped Samuels hobble through the slurry of stinking, rotting straw and hay, the array of strong odours assailing them from all directions. Amy, swallowing down the bile, brushed sweat from her brow and reached out a hand to push open the stable door.

A man stood there, his impressive bulk nothing but a large, looming black shape in the doorway, blocking their exit. Amy almost squealed and reeled backwards, Samuels groaning in her embrace. How had Kestler managed to find her, to follow her at this exact point in time? Was he like that magician she had seen in the theatre one time. What was he called? A mind-reader? Hypnotist? She couldn't quite recall, remembering only how Stacey had laughed so loudly. The last time he had done so, she recalled. Maybe this was to be her last time also. Her last time for anything.

'You'd do best to keep quiet,' said the man. It wasn't Kestler's voice, she knew that. He stepped in close and shot out his left fist straight into Samuel's face, felling him like a tree. He lifted the injured man with ease, draping him over his broad shoulders. 'Stay close.'

'But who are you?'

'Don't you worry about that,' he said. 'I'll get us out of this mess.'

'My buggy's over yonder,' she said, pointing vaguely to her left.

'We won't be needing your buggy,' he said.

She froze at his words, taking a moment to find the courage to say, 'Why not?'

'Because,' he said, drawing his gun and easing back the hammer ominously, 'we're going to visit Mr Kestler and he's gonna reward me handsomely for putting paid to your little scheme.'

'You can't. For the love of God, you can't!'

He pressed the muzzle against her forehead, 'Oh yes I can, little missy. I need to get back into his good books, and this is the perfect way to do it. Now, walk ahead and make straight for his store. One false move and I'll put a bullet in your spine.'

'You miserable cur.'

The big man chuckled. 'I've been called a lot worse, little missy, but that'll suit me just fine. Now walk on, I'm tired and I want this done.'

Someone was talking as they came through the doors of Kestler's mercantile store. The voice sounded raucous, words delivered with deliberate slowness. 'I need those guarantees, Mr Lomax. I need them by tomorrow so I can ...' The voice drifted away as the speaker, standing behind the counter, with the earpiece clamped hard against the side of his head, saw the intruders and reached for something hidden underneath. 'I'll call you back Mr Lomax ... No, I will call *you back*!' He replaced the earpiece on its cradle and levelled the revolver he'd taken from its hiding place towards the three strange looking characters advancing upon him through the murkiness of the store. 'Y'all just hold on right there,' he said.

'Name's Soloman,' came the voice of the large man holding another over his shoulder. 'I'm here to speak with Mr Kestler.'

'I know who you are,' said the man as he moved from behind the counter and stepped through the open hatch, gun in hand, eyes narrowed. 'What is it you want, Soloman.'

'I want to talk to Mr Kestler. I have some things to tell him, and these two here might give me some leverage. I upset Mr Kestler, let him down with my boys. They were green, made mistakes. I don't make mistakes and these here are my proof.' Grunting, he lay his burden on the ground.

'Who is she?'

Soloman lifted his head, sensing Amy trembling beside him. 'She was gonna help this one get away. Said she wanted to make Kestler pay for what he did.'

The man with the gun was close now. Tall, well dressed, he studied Amy, running his eyes over her, pursing his lips. 'I believe you had a dinner date with our mutual friend. Mrs Childer isn't it?'

'Hardly a friend, whoever you are.'

'Name is Haynes. They call me Doc Haynes, on account I used to look after people's feet back in San Francisco.'

'*Feet?*' Soloman blurted, unable to keep his amusement to himself. 'I reckon I've heard everything now.'

'Mr Kestler is in the saloon next door,' said Haynes, his voice turning icy cold. 'My advice is to go and tell him what you told me while I wait here and entertain this little lady.'

Soloman hesitated, rubbing his face with agitation, 'I reckon I'll wait.'

'You'll be waiting a long time, friend. Mr Kestler likes his drink. Best go and talk to him before words of any kind make very little sense to him.'

'I'll take the lady.'

The gun came up, 'No you won't. She'll be just fine here with me.'

An age seemed to pass between them before Soloman gave in, blowing out a long sigh. He swung around and stomped off towards the door. As he opened it, Hayne squeezed off a single shot, the heavy slug hitting Soloman high up in the shoulder, the impact projecting him into the street.

The body made a heavy clump as it landed in the dirt. Amy screamed and Hayne struck her hard across the face, sending her crashing to her knees. 'Why is it always me who has to tidy up the ends of this pathetic little business.'

With the sound of Amy's whimpering filling the store, Haynes prodded Samuels with the toe of his boot. He ejected the spent cartridge from his Remington and slipped another into the cylinder.

Approaching voices caused him to look up and all at once a gaggle of loud, well-armed men erupted through the doors, headed by a reeling Kestler. 'What is all the shootin', Doc?'

'We've had a visitor.' Haynes nodded towards Amy still on her knees, head down. 'Seems like Mrs Childer here wanted to rescue your prisoner. Soloman found 'em and brought them to us, hoping he could ingratiate himself back into your good books.'

'Well, he did for his two idiot partners,' mumbled Kestler, approaching none too steadily. 'But even so, I can't trust him, not after this. Where is he?'

'Outside. I sent him on his way with a bullet in his back. Get one of the boys to finish him off.'

'Outside?'

'Yeah. In the street. It's a surprise you didn't see him.'

Troubled, Kestler snapped his fingers, 'Rogers, go and take a look.'

Rogers, chomping on a bone pipe, mumbled something inaudible and went through the main door. It wasn't long before he came back in. 'Ain't no one there, Mr Kestler.'

Kestler snapped his head around to Doc Haynes, who pushed through them all.

Outside, in the dark, he could just about make out the imprint of where Soloman's heavy body had hit the ground.

But of Soloman himself, there was no sign.

CHAPTER NINETEEN

Kestler sat in his saloon, turning a half-filled glass of whisky between his palms, staring at the dishevelled Amy Childer sitting opposite him. Standing at his shoulder was Doc Haynes, tapping his foot impatiently. 'She was going to skedaddle before Soloman waylaid her. She'd have ridden over to El Paso, warned the authorities. We don't need U.S. Marshalls snooping around. We can ill-afford any—'

'*All right, I hear you!*' Kestler rocked forward and threw the whisky down his throat. As the fiery liquid percolated through his guts, he grew calmer. 'I hear you. What do you suggest?'

'Kill her, bury the body out in the prairie. Coyotes will get rid of any evidence.'

Amy squirmed in her chair, the only sound emanating from her mouth a muffled squeak. Her jaw and mouth were swollen to twice their normal size, a vicious looking bruise of deepest purple covering the lower half of her face.

'What about the husband?'

They both looked up to Bart Owens, standing there, toying with Roose's gun.

'What about him?' asked Haynes. 'From what I hear, he's a drunk. He won't even notice she's gone.'

'But what if he does?'

Haynes and Kestler exchanged a look. 'Mitch,' said Kestler, 'take a ride over there, make sure Mr Childer won't say anything to anyone.'

Tipping his hat, Mitch Rogers put his bone pipe into his waistcoat pocket, turned, and left without a word.

'Mr Kestler,' said Owens, appearing awkward, unable to look Kestler in the eye, 'I have to say … Some of the boys, they is mighty edgy with them Comanch around the place.'

'*Them Comanch*,' put in Haynes quickly, 'have served us well. I been through what they took and it amounts to a fair amount. My contacts in San Francisco will ensure us of a good return.'

'Bart,' said Kestler, rising unsteadily to his feet, 'I know you have read all them dime novels about how Comanches roamed the plains, butchering men, women and children, but those days have gone.'

'With all due respect, Mr Kestler, they is old, and from the *old days*. They is as much a bunch of murdering savages as any who ever rode all them years ago.'

'Ah, Bart, are you listening to yourself? We are living in the modern world right now. Those days have gone. There ain't no more savages torching houses and raping females. They are civilised.' He weaved his way between tables and and reached the bar, out of breath, squeezing finger and thumb into his eyes. 'Hot diggity, I don't feel so good.'

'You should ease off the juice,' said Haynes.

'It's late,' said Kestler, ignoring his partner's jibe. 'I'm going to bed. Bart,' he swung around to level his bleary, bloodshot eyes on the tall, lean gunman. 'Take her out into the prairie and finish her, just as Doc suggests. Watch out for coyotes.'

'But Brody and those Comanch are out there.'

'*Don't answer me back, Owens*!' Kestler took in a shuddering breath. 'Just do as you're told.'

Pulling a face, Owens reluctantly took hold of Amy by the shoulder and hauled her to her feet, ramming the gun into her back. He pushed her through the batwing doors and they both disappeared into the early morning darkness.

They camped amongst the rocks, Scarface lighting a fire around which they huddled. Roose, trussed up so well he could barely move, watched them keenly. Brody, some way off, stood staring out across the plain. If Roose could somehow manage to loosen the leather thongs which bound his wrists and ankles, he could perhaps overcome one of them, take their gun, kill Brody. The rest would run. He was sure of that.

As sure as he was that any idea of escape was futile.

He put his head back against the cold rocks. These men were experts. There was little chance of him loosening his bindings. He'd been trying unsuccessfully to do so since the moment one of the Indians secured his limbs together. Nothing gave then, nothing gave now. It was useless and he cursed himself for not making a fight of it back in the town. True, he'd be dead, but he'd take some of those curs with him. His predicament now could only result in one outcome. His head dropped to his chest, despair engulfing him. If he could see Maddie one more time, then none of this would seem so bad. A fool he was for leaving her. A fool for coming out here on this mad errand. A fool for not waiting for Cole to recover. Together, they could have put them all into the ground. Fate had worked against him, as always. Damn this hopeless situation and this accursed life.

Something caused Stone to turn over and sit up from his bedroll, senses alert. A movement in the darkness, the glint of eyes shining bright as candles in the night. With extreme care, he reached out for his revolver and eased back the hammer. A coyote, perhaps more than one, circling him. He should have made a fire, but fear of being seen prevented him from doing so. Perhaps that was a mistake.

He swept his hand across the ground, found a small rock and climbed to his feet, ready to open fire if one of the coyotes attacked. He launched the rock towards the eyes. A yelp, followed by the desperate retreat of the animal and once again, Stone was alone.

Releasing a long sigh, he relaxed and went to return to his makeshift bed when he saw something out the corner of his eye. A light, way over to the west. This time it burned from no animal. Moving across to an outcrop of boulders, he heaved himself to the top and peered through the night. A campfire. Unmistakeable. Whoever it was had revealed their position, just as he had avoided doing so. He gave up a small prayer of thanks. Could it be Roose, returning from his meeting with Kestler? With no way of knowing, all he could do was wait. Something unwanted stirred inside, however. A feeling, a suspicion that perhaps it wasn't Roose. Perhaps men, sent by Kestler to track Stone down. Uneasily, he slinked back to his camp and hurriedly rolled up his blankets. He'd ride back to Reuben Cole's without delay. If it was Roose, then that would be all to the good, but if not ... Gritting his teeth, he worked feverishly and soon, with his horse well packed, he set off at a steady pace across the wide-open prairie, the approaching dawn nothing but a light grey smudge on the distant horizon.

Bacon rind and grits sizzled in a blackened pan, whilst Brody, stretching out his limbs, instructed two of his companions to bring Roose forward.

'We have no time to play with you, my friend,' said Brody as the others cut through Roose's bindings and pulled off his jacket and shirt. His lily white body shivered in the cold, morning light. Soon, as the sun rose, the temperature too would increase. His skin would blister and burn. He stood, limp, defeated, as they cut through his trousers and left him quivering there, like a plucked turkey, ready for the pot.

Slowly, Brody drew out his broad-bladed Bowie. He tested the edge with his thumb and hissed. 'How many of you were there, my friend, hunting us?'

Roose's eyes came up, dark, defiant. He may well have accepted his fate but he was damned if he was going to tell this monster anything at all. Grinning, Brody nodded to his men, who held onto Roose by the arms and legs. Four men, all of them cackling like febrile, malicious children, impatient for the sport to begin.

Brody moved up close, the blade before his face. 'You will tell me, just like your friend did.'

Roose wanted to scream. So, they'd overtaken Stone. The game was up.

'So why not save yourself some pain, eh? Or do you like pain?' Roose muttered something, shaking his head once. 'No, of course not. But *this* pain, it is going to be like nothing you have ever experienced before.' Taking his time, Brody placed the blade flat against Roose's withered stomach and gently lowered it towards his manhood. He continued, all the while his eyes locked on Roose's, whose teeth chattered as the true horror of what was about to happen struck home.

Turning the blade, Brody rested the tip against Roose's rectum.

'I'll ask you one more time, my friend. How many men came with you, and where are they now?'

Roose merely glared.

Brody pushed and the accompanying scream rang out across the plain louder than any thunderclap.

Flat on his ample belly, Soloman looked down from his vantage point to where Brody and his men were just putting the finishing touches to their torture of Sterling Roose. Rolling over, he looked to the sky for a moment, ran a calloused hand over his face and sat up. Across from where he was, Amy Childer sat with her back against a blackened tree, the tears cutting through the grime of her pretty face.

'This ain't gonna end well for anyone,' Soloman said and stood up. He waddled over to her and flopped down on the ground. 'Listen, what I did by knocking out that S.O.B down back there, rescuing you, that means they'll be coming for me, to kill me.' He rolled his shoulder and winced. 'Lucky for me that bullet only winged me. Two times I been shot here, and two times the bullet has not stuck. That ain't nothing unusual. I've mostly been lucky my whole life. And now I've met you.'

Her eyes came up. There was malevolence in her look, determination too. 'If you believe you are any better than those ghastly men of Kestler's, you've got another think coming, mister. I thank you for knocking that scoundrel down the way you did, but I also know that other one went to kill my Stacey. My life has no future now, so you may as well kill me and get it over with.'

He gaped at her. 'Kill you? Why would I wanna do that? Nah, I ain't gonna kill you. Listen, I think if you take me to your place, we can hole up there for a while, then I'll make my plans.'

'You're not holin' up anywhere that has anything to do with me, mister.'

'So I just cut you adrift, is that it? You sure is unappreciative of my kindness.'

'Your kindness? You were gonna turn me over to Kestler and let him do whatever he wanted until you realised he would cut you no deal. You're all the same – murderers, cheats and scoundrels the lot of you!'

'You sure are some kinda wildcat. I like that in a woman.'

She snapped her head away, fresh tears tumbling down her face. 'Shoot me. That's the only thing I want from you.'

'Well, it ain't gonna be the only thing you get.'

She looked at him, horrified. 'No. Please, I'm begging you ...'

'I can't figure you, woman. One minute you're begging me to shoot you dead, next thing you is resisting my advances. What is it you want exactly?'

'To go back home. Bury my husband, then leave this godforsaken place once and for all.'

'On your own? Ma'am, this may be the twentieth century an' all, but from what I've just witnessed, there is still plenty of mean individuals roaming this land. Best if you go home and wait for me.'

'Wait for you?'

'Why not? It's a good proposition. I will look after you, treat you well ...' He winked. 'And satisfy you, I can guarantee you that.'

'You think a lot of yourself, don't you.'

'Ma'am, from where I'm sitting, you don't have much choice. I would love to share my life with you, settle down, maybe build up a business. Kestler has given me some ideas to work on so this all might just work out well in the end.'

She considered him for a long time. 'All right. I can see you are a man of talent, unlike Stacey who drinks himself into a stupor every night. The likelihood he is dead, shot by that stringy one with the pipe. Crazy thing is, I couldn't care less. My life has been going nowhere fast these past years, perhaps I do need a new direction.'

'I'll give you any number of directions, I promise you.'

After she'd provided him with basic directions to her homestead, she scurried away whilst he, checking his guns, swung in behind Brody and his men, careful to keep his distance, sure they would be winding their way back to Reuben Cole's now they had finalised their business with their prisoner. Both they and Soloman needed Cole dead, for he was a heap of trouble and once he knew his partner was dead, vengeance would drive him relentlessly on, like one of the steam engines dissecting the prairie and opening it up to the modern world. He'd have to die, decided Soloman. Brody and his men too.

CHAPTER TWENTY

Stone spotted the dust cloud as he gained the ridge. They were a considerable distance from him, but there could be no mistake. Whoever had lit the campfire was coming his way. Pursuing him. From the amount of dust, he knew there were more than one, so that ruled our Roose. And they were riding fast. He wished he had Roose's field glasses to pick out just who they were. Cursing his bad luck, he spurred his horse and broke her into a gallop, heading for the only place to go he felt safest – Reuben Cole's.

Sitting out on his sprawling veranda, Cole stared across the vast landscape bordering his ranch. Since the previous day, he felt restless, stomping around the big house aimlessly, ignoring the pleadings of Maddie to rest. 'I've done enough resting,' he told her and spent a lot of time cleaning his guns, checking his saddle and bridle, ensuring his canteens and grain sacks were prepared and ready.

'You're not going out there,' she said, stepping onto the veranda. Her sleeves were rolled up, a scarlet scarf tied around her head, face flush with exertion.

'What you been doin' in there?'

'Cleaning. Not sure who that woman was who you had coming in, but there is a lot of work to do to get this place straight.'

He smiled, despite the heaviness he felt in his heart. 'You don't need to do any of that, Maddie.'

'Sure I do,' she said, coming over and sitting down on his lap. She snaked her arms around his neck and kissed him passionately. 'You need a woman to look after you, Cole.'

'Well, I'm hoping I've found one.'

They kissed again, but suddenly she tensed and pulled back, troubled. 'When will we tell Sterling?'

Shifting position, Cole looked away, awkward, uncomfortable. 'I don't know. It's gonna be just about the most difficult thing I've ever done.'

'Worse than hunting Indians?'

'Much worse,' he said without hesitation. 'He's my only true friend. I know how much you mean to him.'

'It's not something either of us planned, Cole.'

'I know that. Don't make it any easier though.'

She put her head on his shoulder, caressing the back of his scalp, and they both drifted off into their own, private thoughts.

At first, looking up a few moments later, Cole believed the swirl of dust was a mere devil, kicked up by the wind which often came out of nowhere to assault the ground. As he focused in, he realised it was an approaching rider. He patted Maddie's arm. 'Go into the study, Maddie, get yourself a Winchester from the rack.'

Stiffening, she sat up and followed his gaze. 'It could be Sterling.'

'It could, but he's galloping as if the hounds of hell were on his tail.' He reached down to his side and picked up his own repeating rifle and levered a cartridge into the breach. 'Fetch that gun and stay indoors.'

Sensing his tension, Maddie immediately disappeared inside and Cole stood up.

He waited, all of his attention on the rider.

It was not Roose. Absent were the tell-tale black frock coat and the battered old Stetson that Sterling always wore. This rider was bareheaded, dressed in a pale blue shirt and denim trousers.

Dropping to one knee, Cole flipped up the fold-down rear sight and squinted along the length of the barrel until he had the rider in his view. He gave a start as the man drew closer. '*Stone,*' he gasped and stood up.

Stone pulled his mount up sharply, the horse kicking and neighing, eyes wide with alarm, nostrils flared. The young man jumped down before the dust had settled and raced up to Cole.

'They're coming, Mr Cole. Five of 'em.'

'Coming? Who's coming?'

'The men who ... Ahh, I have to say it, Mr Cole.' Without warning, the tears sprang from his eyes and he slumped down on the bottom step which led to the veranda. Holding nothing back, his pent-up emotions burst forth like the waters from a broken dam. Pressing his face in his hands, he wept uncontrollably.

'Son,' said Cole quietly, sitting down next to him. He gently slipped his arm around Stone's shoulders. 'Try and tell me what in tarnation is going on.'

Battling to suppress his body-jerking sobs, Stone eventually brought his head up, gulping in air, calming himself down. 'Mr Roose and me made to go into the town. Lawrenceville. Mr Samuels, he said he couldn't be involved in any killing, so he left. But then, as we moved down towards the town, we saw the Indians. Comanch, I think. They had Mr Samuels with 'em. Mr Roose, he became ... I don't know how to explain it, but he changed. Already he'd ...' Stone squeezed his eyes shut. 'Cougan, you remember him?'

'I do. His pa rode with us years before.'

'He ... Mr Cole, I ain't ever seen anything like what happened. Cougan got real agitated when Mr Samuels said he was coming back here. Cougan drew a knife and was gonna kill poor Mr Samuels—'

'He was gonna *what*?'

'It's true, I swear to you. But Mr Roose, he just came up behind him and put his own knife deep into Cougan's back, killed him right there and then. Then, he just lay right down there on the ground and went to sleep, as if nothing had happened.'

Cole shifted his eyes towards the open range. 'Sterling has been acting kinda strange these past months. Like he's losing control of his senses.'

'I heard it said that sort of thing often happens to old folk. But Mr Roose ain't so very old, is he?'

Cole didn't answer, merely blew out a breath. 'Carry on with the story, son.'

'Well, when we saw them riding down with Mr Samuels, Mr Roose told me to come back here, tell you to send for soldiers and go into Lawrenceville and arrest that Kestler. Then he went there.'

'Sterling went into the town?' Stone nodded, sniffing loudly. 'To take on Kestler on his own?'

'That was his idea, I think. He said he was gonna just talk, persuade Kestler to let Mr Samuels go. But ... Mr Cole, he was different. He was cold. Like he was someplace else.'

'Shoot,' said Cole, rubbing his face, thinking hard. 'He was setting to kill him. I know that from the old days, how Sterling would become like a man possessed.'

'There's something else.'

Cole nodded. 'I thought there might be.'

'They're following me. Those Comanch. They've been on my trail all night and day. I've led 'em straight to you, Mr Cole.'

Then something curious happened.

A grin spread out across Cole's face. 'That's just about the best thing you could have done, son.' He turned to the young rider. 'You take that big Sharps gun of yours and get up on the balcony with Maddie. When I give the signal, you pour down lead into those renegades until there ain't no more of 'em left standing.'

'What will you do?'

Cole stood up, put the Winchester over his shoulder, and smiled again. 'I'm gonna give them the biggest shock of their lives.'

From where they reined in their horses, the large house appeared deserted. Scarface crossed his hands on the pommel of his saddle and leaned forward. 'He must be inside.'

'Tracks tell us he came this way,' said another, reading the signs in the dirt.

'Then we'll just have to go inside and fetch him out,' said Brody. He smiled at the others. 'Once we have him, we can search through the house and take anything Soloman left behind. Mr Kestler will be more than pleased.'

'He has yet to pay us,' said Scarface with meaning.

'He will have no worries about that.' He studied the upper storey and something about it made him wary. 'I'm not sure, but I think maybe he is in there, watching.'

'Watching?' Scarface drew his revolver. 'Let's just go inside and kill the old coot.'

Brody grunted his assent and edged his horse forward.

From the balcony, Maddie and Stone rose to their knees from their prone positions and opened up on the Indians, the fusillade deafening and almost continuous.

Screaming out orders above the tumult, Brody reeled his horse away, returning fire into the balcony from his Colt with wild, unaimed shots. A heavy slug tore into the Indian beside him, flinging him to the ground. Another screamed, bullets peppering his chest. 'Spread out,' shouted Brody, frantically kicking his horse's flanks, whilst his other two companions dispersed in the opposite direction.

As he struggled to control his incensed mount, Brody stared into his fastly approaching death.

A horse came thundering from the far flank, pounding across the ground, on a collision course with Brody and his men. He gawped in disbelief, not knowing what to do, uncertain why the horse would be charging with such determination. Such control.

Soon, within a few blinks, he saw the reason.

A man, hidden from view by pressing himself flat against the far side of his horse's flank, rose up into the saddle, the Winchester aiming, firing. Measured shots, some going wide due to the horse's jolting forward momentum, but enough striking home to throw the remaining Comanches from their saddles as they desperately tried to get away.

Cole threw the spent Winchester to the ground, drew his Cavalry Colt from his cross-belly holster and put a bullet into Brody's right shoulder, pitching him over the back of his horse, which reared up, screaming, and bolted across the dried, hard-packed ground.

'Cole!'

Steadying his horse, Cole circled around the writhing body of his would-be assailant, and looked up to see Maddie standing on the balcony, bare forearm pressed against her brow. 'Cole, for pity's sake ...'

'It's all right,' he spat and dropped from his saddle.

Brody squirmed, blood pumping from the ghastly wound high up in his chest. His own revolver lay tantalisingly close but, as his feverish eyes locked upon it, Cole kicked it further out of reach. He eased back the hammer of his gun. 'What did you do to my friend?'

From somewhere, amidst the sea of pain washing over him, Brody grew aware of Cole's voice. The words. Their meaning. He forced a grin. 'Go stuff yourself,' he said.

Running his tongue across his lips, Cole shook his head and returned the Colt to its holster. 'Problem is, boy, I rode down scum like you across this land a quarter of a century ago, so I know all about your ways. I know you would have taken great delight in torturing my friend.' He nodded at Brody's bowie knife sheathed at his hip. 'You would have used that, splitting my friend from stem to stern. I seen it. I know it. And now,' he paused for effect before reaching behind him to pull out his own heavy-bladed knife, some twelve inches of cold steel long, 'now, the same is gonna happen to you.'

'I will not tell you anything, gringo.'

'Oh yes you will,' said Cole, 'you'll tell me everything.'

Within five minutes of setting to work, Cole learned everything he needed to know. He didn't hear Maddie's screams or see Stone throwing up. He didn't hear or see anything. Only what Brody said. And then Cole split the man open and let him bleed out in the burning sun of a that long, awful day.

'Burn the bodies,' Cole told Stone afterwards, rechecking his weapons and rolling up his bed blanket. 'Then, go into town and send a telegram to the Army over in Carson City, tell 'em what is going on down in Lawrenceville. That Kestler is bankrolling his shares in the railroad by stealing valuables from the big houses surrounding Freedom. You think you can do that?'

'Sure I can, Mr Cole. I'll use the telephone. It'll be quicker.'

'Good,' said Cole. The quicker the better, he thought to himself. He had no idea how many men Kestler had working for him. He'd need all of his wits about him, as well as all of his skills. Despite the bruising and aching joints from the initial burglary causing him a lot less discomfort, a tiny doubt lingered. The attack on Brody and his Comanche associates had taken a lot out of him. No matter how difficult it was to admit it to himself, he knew age was against him. Riding on his horse in the old Apache way had seriously taken it out of him. His back had all tightened up and his thighs burned like they were sat in a pail of steaming hot water.

'You can't go,' said Maddie, appearing as if from nowhere, her eyes wet with tears. 'I'm begging you, Cole. You can't.'

'I have to,' he said without looking up from his preparations. 'You know that.'

'I don't know any such thing! You go down there alone, you'll end up dead, Just like Sterling.'

Cole stopped tying up his bedroll and bit his lip. 'That precisely why I have to go, Maddie. He was my friend. To die like that ...' He shook his head a swallowed down the rising grief. 'I'm gonna make them pay for what they did. It's what I have to do.'

'If you get back, you stubborn old mule, I won't be here.'

He turned his face up and stared into her wet beautiful eyes. 'Yes you will.'

'No I won't, damn you!' She flew into him, her fists beating at his chest, the tears cascading down her cheeks. 'I can't lose both of you.'

He went to hold her, to press her to him, to bring her some comfort and reassurance. Violently, she tore herself free, features twisted into a mask of pure, raging fury. 'I swear it, if you go, I will leave.'

They held one another's stares for a long time before Cole gathered up his belongings and strode outside to his waiting horse. Aware she was standing there, glaring at his back, he nevertheless steeled himself not to turn around. Instead, he hauled himself into the saddle and gently eased his horse out across the range towards the town of Lawrenceville and the reckoning which awaited them all.

CHAPTER TWENTY-ONE

The town proved not as busy as he had expected. True, there were people around, shops open, the livery stable and merchandise stores doing a brisk trade, but there was something missing. Friendliness, warmth, call it what you will, these things did not feature in the downcast and unhappy faces of the populace. At its heart, there was a tangible indifference, an acceptance of their lot. This was not a happy place.

There were two men sitting outside the first saloon Cole came to, hats pulled down over their faces, legs, encased in knee-high riding boots, stretched out, their tied down guns declaring to the world exactly who they were. Swallowing down his rising anger, Cole got down from his horse and tied the reins to the hitching post. This was a little like stepping back in time. The lawlessness that once clung to the West seemed to have found its last stronghold in this dreary, uninviting town.

As he clumped up the steps towards the double batwing doors, both men roused themselves and regarded him with icy stares. He tipped his hat and went inside.

Being late afternoon there were few customers inside. A couple of other gunslingers were at a round table playing cards, bored expressions on their faces, cigarette smoke hanging over them in ominous clouds. A half bottle of whisky sat in the centre of the table, a sprinkling of dollar coins splayed around it. A woman wearing a tight bodice of the brightest scarlet looked up from her position astride one of the gunslinger's laps and gave Cole a smile. The man followed her gaze. He did not smile.

As Cole went directly to the bar. He heard the exchange of comments from the card playing table. At the same time through the doors stepped the two from outside. Cole closed his eyes, doing his damndest to stay calm. He did not yet seek a confrontation, but being intimidated might just put the flame to the fuse. Blowing out a long sigh, he caught the barkeeper's eye. 'Do you serve coffee?'

'We serve anything you want, stranger.'

'Black coffee.'

Nodding, the barkeeper moved to the far end of the bar to prepare the order and Cole heard them coming closer.

Two from the table, two from the doors.

He kept his eyes fixed firmly ahead and could see them clearly in the long mirror on the wall behind the counter.

'That's a mighty fine rig you're wearing, mister,' said one of them.

Cole turned and studied the man sidling up to him. Tall and gangly, at his waist, a well worn Remington New Model Police revolver in a tooled holster, arranged for a cross-belly draw. It was Roose's gun. Cole kept his growing fury to himself, the almost debilitating urge to reach over and snuff out the man's life difficult to control. But he managed it. Instead of killing the man, he shrugged. He too sported a cross-belly rig. 'Could be we're twins.'

The others laughed, but the tall guy frowned. 'What's your business here, mister?'

Ignoring the threatening tone, Cole felt some relief as the barkeeper returned with his coffee. He took a sip and nodded in appreciation. 'That's good.'

'I asked you a question.'

'Well ...' Cole replaced the cup on its saucer and turned it around, aware of the man's impatience and liking it. 'I'm passing through.'

'Passing through to where?'

'Home.' The others were not joining in, allowing the gangly one to do all the talking. Perhaps the baiting might increase shortly, so Cole took his time, trying to ease the tension. He said, as calmly as he could, 'Friend, you seem awful agitated. Have I done something to offend you? If I have, then I apologise.'

The one on his left cleared his throat, 'Yeah, come on Bart, let's leave it now, huh.'

'On your way home,' said Bart, brushing aside his comrade's words. 'And where's home?'

'Tucson. Left the army about a month ago, and I'm taking my time riding the range for one last time.'

'Left the army?'

'Yes, sir. I've been a scout for them for the past thirty years or so, but my time has ended. Fort Concho will be closing soon, now that the frontier is tamed.'

'Is that what you did, mister?' asked the one on his left. A younger man, his youthful face glowed with impish curiosity. 'You were out fighting Indians and all?'

'I did, yes. But that was some time ago.'

Another man leaned forward, 'What do you make of that Buffalo Bill and his Wild West Show?'

Cole chuckled and finished his coffee. 'Is that what it's called? I wouldn't know.'

Leaning across the counter on his right elbow, Bart appeared more serious than ever. 'So what do you make of him, that Buffalo Bill? You had dealings with him?'

'Not as such, no. Saw him from a distance once, many years ago. I never did consider him as anything more than an opportunist.'

'An oppor-what?' asked the young one.

Cole looked at him. 'Maybe not him directly, but people like him ripped the very heart out of the Indian by what they done.'

'How they do that?'

'They took away their means to live. Their relationship with the buffalo goes back way beyond when the White Man first came into this land, but we saw fit to destroy them. Or, at least, try to. The Indian lived with the buffalo, used its meat, its fur. Even its sinews. All the White Man did was cut off its hide and leave its flesh to rot out in the prairie.'

'Sounds like you're an Indian-lover, mister.'

Cole gave Bart a dismissive glance. 'If we hadn't taken away their soul, their way of life, we would not have had all the troubles we've had, and none of the killing.'

'All because of killing the buffalo?'

'Mainly, in my view.'

'But you fought Indians?' said the young one. 'You knew them for what they were. Murdering scum.' The others grunted in agreement. 'I have heard some more broke out of the reservation. Comanche.'

'They should all be strung up,' said Bart through his teeth. 'They ain't nothing more than animals.'

'I take it you've never met one? Face to face, I mean. Talked. Tried to understand 'em?'

'And you have?'

Cole nodded. 'On many occasions.'

Bart turned away and spat into the spittoon at his feet. 'Like I said, an Indian-lover.'

'I don't excuse what they have done, to settlers and the like,' Cole continued unabated, 'but I do understand it. You take away wood from a carpenter, what's he gonna do? Become a farmer? After a lifetime of making things with his hands … It's the same with the Indians. The *Lords of the Southern Plains* is what they called the Comanche. But that was back then when this was their land. Now it's ours, but at least the buffalo is coming back.' He pushed himself away from the counter and stretched his back. 'Do you know of anywhere that has rooms?'

The barkeeper, to whom Cole spoke, wiped his hands on his apron. 'Penny Albright has rooms. You'll find her two streets down on the right of the Crosskeys Mercantile Bank.'

Cole tipped his hat and placed a dollar on the counter. 'Keep the change.'

'I thought you was passing through?'

Turning his smile to Bart, Cole regarded the man's rig, deciding there and then he would be the first to die. 'I'll need a good night's rest first. Then, after a hearty breakfast, I'll be on my way.' He nodded to each in turn. 'I'll be seeing you.'

He left, pushing through the batwings and stood to scan the town. The gunslingers moved close up behind him, their spurs pinging loudly in the quiet saloon interior. Without a backward glance, Colt went to his horse and eased himself into the saddle.

He found the boarding house without much trouble.

Penny Albright was not what Cole was expecting. He didn't exactly know *what* he was expecting, but the trim, middle-aged woman with a strikingly beautiful face and green eyes that twinkled mischievously who greeted him when he called was certainly not it!

She showed him to his room, which was small, bright, and furnished with a good deal of comfort and cleanliness. A sudden urge to jump on the bed and bounce up and down on the mattress gripped him, but he managed to remain standing, drinking her in. He checked her hand and saw she wore a ring. What's more, she noticed him checking and he blushed.

'My husband is a surveyor, Mister ...?'

'Cole. Reuben Cole.'

'Are you feeling all right, Mr Cole? You seem somewhat pinky.'

'Pinky?' He felt along his jawline, the heat still there from his blushing. 'No, no, I'm fine.'

'No, I meant the bruising.'

'Ah!' He forced a laugh, his discomfort growing by the second. He slumped down on the bed, suddenly tired, the pain in his ribs returning with a vengeance. He pressed his hand against his right side without thinking. Her expression grew more concerned. 'I, er, had an accident out on the range. Nothing serious.'

'You look tuckered out if you don't mind me saying, Mr Cole. I shall bring you a hot meal to your room so as you do not need to go downstairs. I have only one other guest, a travelling salesman out of Kansas City. He too will be leaving in the morning.'

'It's a busy little town then?'

She went to speak, then pressing her lips together, stopped herself. He frowned. 'It used to be a *good* little town, Mr Cole. Until certain unsavoury elements came here and made their presence felt. A lot of people have since left.'

'Ah, yes. I think I met a few in the saloon when I first arrived.'

'Gunmen?' He nodded and again became aware of her eyes settling on his own handgun. 'That perhaps is something you know a lot about, Mr Cole?'

'I'm an army scout, ma'am. Ex-army. I've ridden across every square inch of this territory and men like those in the saloon have been my companions for way too long.'

'Not friendly companions I hope.'

'Indeed not, ma'am. I have little truck with men such as those. What exactly are they doing here, do you know?'

'They are the employees of a man called Kestler. Randolph Kestler. I shall not go into the details, for he is a man of un-Christian habits and has brought no end of spite and malice to Lawrenceville. He has shares in the railroad and is looking to expand the tracks further into New Mexico and beyond, gaining profit from the transportation of steers. He has made huge investments and courted the avarice of cattle barons from right down to the Mexican border. For them to trust him with moving their herds, he would need an orderly town and many have sprung up all along the railroad, but not many are made *orderly* in the way this one is.'

'I see.'

'I'm not sure you do, Mr Cole.'

'He's a businessman, looking to develop his company.'

'A businessman who develops his company by raising money using any means he can to get it.'

'Dishonestly, you mean?'

She pursed her lips, clearly in some discomfort with discussing all of this with a perfect stranger. Cole understood and did not press the point. How was she to know who he was? In all reality, he could even be another employee of Kestler's, sent to sound out public opinion. He sighed and stood up, throwing down his hat and pulling off his coat. He winced as a stab of pain shot through him and she hurried to his side and helped him.

'You need rest, Mr Cole.'

'Thank you, Mrs Albright.'

She watched him as he stretched himself out on the bed.

Within a blink, he was fast asleep.

CHAPTER TWENTY-TWO

The wind whipped tiny dust devils in the main street and the horses tied to the hitching rails scraped at the ground, whinnying in discomfort as tiny shards of gravel slapped into their faces or heavier pieces stung their rumps.

Kestler, sitting on his rocking chair smoking a large cigar, stood up and stretched himself out. 'Storm coming,' he said to nobody in particular.

He went to turn away and go back inside. The promise of a hot meal and a glass of bourbon in front of the fire was extremely seductive, but something made him stop. He slowly turned, half expecting to see nothing but the horses all jittery, longing to be inside a stable. Instead, he saw a man. Tall, dressed in buckskin coat and long boots, a bandana covering most of his face, the broad-brimmed straw hat fluttering so strongly it looked as if it might take off at any moment.

'Can I help you, stranger?'

'Could be.' He pulled down the bandana to reveal his craggy features, hard as flint.

Something about the voice, the steel in it, caused Kestler to tense up. He did not flinch as somebody moved behind him.

Bart Owens stepped up next to his boss. 'Who's this?'

'I don't know.'

Owens cleared his throat and took a step forward. 'Hey, I know you. I met you last night. You was looking for a room. If you're looking for something else, we ain't got—'

'Roose Sterling.'

'Who—'

Kestler put a warning arm on Bart's arm. 'Go get the boys, Bart.'

Something passed between them and Bart, picking up on the fear in his boss's voice, whirled and half-ran back inside.

'I don't know where he is,' said Kestler, rolling his shoulders, placing his thumbs in his waistband, inches from his revolver, 'if that's what you're asking.'

'Sure you do.'

Without warning the wind dropped, as suddenly as it had started, and the relief from the horses was palpable. The tension inside Kestler, however, went up several notches. 'I said I don't.'

The man remained silent, even as four others appeared on the porch, stamping their boots, glowing in anger. Perhaps their card game had been interrupted, or their drinking. Perhaps both. Clearly, whatever the reason, their temper was up and they were red-faced and itching for a fight.

'I'll have to ask you to leave, mister. People like you ain't welcome in this town. And,' a quick glance to the others, 'as it's *my* town, I have the authority.' He leaned forward, jutting out his chin, 'So get the hell out.'

'Is that what you said to Sterling before you ran him out, and fed him to those savages?'

Blinking, Kestler straightened himself up. 'What savages?'

'Around five of 'em. They took Sterling, split him in two before they pegged him out and cooked him in the noonday sun. Next, you'll be telling me you didn't have anything to do with it.'

'I didn't. Who are you, mister?'

'Thing is,' the stranger rubbed his chin, 'I went to the reservation before I came here. Spoke to a few people there. It's kinda unusual for Comanch, or any of 'em, to break out nowadays. No reason. Except ...' His hand dropped, 'except when they'd been offered the chance to make some money.'

Someone whistled faintly. Another coughed nervously. A third made his excuses and went back inside. Kestler never allowed his eyes to leave the stranger. 'I don't know what you're getting at.'

'Is that right? Well, let me enlighten you. You've been employing gangs to purloin various estates around these parts, paying them a pittance against the value of the items they steal. I know.' He pointed inside the big saloon. 'I was in here just last evening. Saw one of my daddy's paintings on your wall in there.'

'*One of your daddy's*...? Mister, my advice, turn around and get out. Now.' He grinned, before giving some added emphasis to his threats, 'Before you get hurt.'

The stranger, however, ignored Kestler's words and continued unabated, with a galling nonchalance. 'My daddy's things, they ain't what brought me back. It's what you did to Sterling. You see, he was a friend and just before I cut out the eyes of the young varmint that led those Comanch, he told me who'd put him up to it.' He rolled his tongue around the inside of his mouth and spat into the dirt. 'It was you, Kestler.'

'Young varmint? Mister, you seem to be cooking up a wild story.'

'Went by the name of Brody.'

The gunhands either side of Kestler stiffened. Bart jutted out his jaw. 'Brody? What did you say you did to him? Cut out his eyes?'

'A lot else besides, after I'd killed those who rode with him.'

'That's hogswill,' said one of the others.

'That's what you'll be soon enough, boy.'

A bone-chilling coldness settled over everything.

Kestler, a big man, ponderous belly sagging over his belt, was confident in his skills. He had killed many men, some, like now, face to face. Something about this man, however, irked him. He had never known anything like this, never gone up against a man such as this. There was something so different about him. A calmness. A latent propensity for violence. The air of danger, of someone of whom he should be wary.

Pushing these doubts and anxieties aside, Kestler gave a laugh and took his chance. He moved, as fast as he could, to draw his gun, but before his fingers had even curled around the butt of his Remington, a bullet struck him between the eyes. He crumpled, not registering anything, and he fell with a colossal crash to the porch floor, sending up a cloud of ancient dust to hover like a shroud over his corpse.

For a moment nobody moved. Everything had happened so quickly. And now Kestler was dead. One minute that well-known sneer, that dismissive arrogance, now nothing remained except an empty husk.

Bart Owens recovered first. He clawed for his gun, the same gun he had taken from Roose, the gun the stranger knew so well. Two bullets slapped into Bart's chest, sending him spinning wildly backwards through the double swing doors to collapse in the saloon. A woman screamed.

The others hesitated.

'He was your boss,' said the stranger, 'he ain't no more. So give it up. You're all out of work.'

He stood with the Colt in his hand, a tiny worm of smoke trailing from the barrel.

For a moment, it seemed nobody would respond, or do the sensible thing. The world stopped. No one spoke or breathed. Then, gradually, the thaw set in. Men's eyes flickered and shoulders relaxed. They exchanged glances and, one by one, they turned away leaving the stranger to consider the body of the dead Kestler. A tiny upturning of one corner of his mouth was his only reaction.

The unmistakable clunk of a revolver's hammer cocking caused Cole to freeze.

'Drop your gun and turn around, nice and slow Mr Cole.'

He did so, the Cavalry hitting the wooden floor with a heavy thump.

'You're darned good, I'll say that for you' said the man. He wore a black waistcoat, white shirt sleeves rolled up past his elbows, spectacles pushed back on top of his head. The gun in his hand barely moved. 'But perhaps your days are over Indian fighter. I doubt I could have crept up on you this easy back when you were out on the plains, hunting down Comanche.'

'Just do what you need to.'

A grin before the man's head erupted in a huge crimson and white ball of blood and brains.

Before the broken corpse toppled to the ground, Cole was diving, hitting the floorboards and rolling over. Sweeping up the Colt Cavalry, he managed to put three rounds towards the man standing some twenty or so paces away in the middle of the street, his Winchester already levering in another cartridge. Head down, Cole drove through what remained of the batwing doors as bullets smacked into the wall either side of him.

He took a moment, eyes fanning over the terrified customers hiding behind upturned tables or cowering in the corners. A gunman with the stem of a white bone pipe sticking out of his shirt pocket scurried over. 'It's Soloman,' he said. 'He put me down just outside Stacey Childer's place. I owe him for that,' he gave emphasis to his words by rubbing the back of his skull.

'This is my fight,' said Cole, taking the chance to reload his gun.

'Don't matter who kills him,' said the pipe-smoker, 'but one of us has to – he ain't gonna stop.' He grinned. 'You've put me out of work, Mr Cole, seeing as you killed both my employers. That one who had the drop on you? He was Kestler's partner, man name of Doc Haynes. Soloman, he's the one who broke into your home. If we help one another, maybe you can let me take my share of the loot they stole.'

'Some of that loot is mine.'

The man raised his hands, 'Hey, I don't mean yours. All I need is enough to set me up in a little tavern down Mexico way. This life ain't for me. I need a change of scenery.' He rubbed the back of his head. 'He hit me so hard, just as I was about to put that poor Childer out of his misery. Least I think it was Soloman. When I came to, everyone had gone. But whatever, I never did like the look of him.'

Another smile and he sprinted towards the doors, bent double, gun in hand. He took a quick glance outside, before rolling out into the open.

Cole followed across the saloon and flattened himself up against the wall adjacent to the shattered doors. Through the splintered woodwork, he managed to watch the man with the pipe scampering around the corner and out of sight.

Two evenly placed Winchester rounds swiftly followed and told him all he needed to know.

He looked back into the saloon. Any remaining people were making a quick and determined exit through the rear door. Beside this was a flight of stairs, leading to several closed rooms, rooms where undoubtedly the whores entertained their customers. Cole ran towards the stairs and took them two at a time.

He tried each door in turn and each one proved to be locked. Cursing, he swung around and shouted down to the barman who was sitting down behind the counter, knees pressed up to his chest, rocking. 'Keys,' he shouted.

The barman looked with vaguely indifferent eyes.

'I want the keys to these doors!'

His only chance of escape, he convinced himself, was to break out through one of the room windows, drop to the street below, and try to outflank the mysterious Soloman. A wild chance, but the only one remaining to him he realized as further measured shots rang out from outside, accompanied by shrieks and cries. He was killing the fleeing customers. The man was incensed. A homicidal maniac. Deranged. Cole sucked in a breath, went up to the first door and kicked at the lock with all his strength.

It splintered but remained firmly closed.

Another kick, then another. Cole, breathing hard, knew he had little time. Another kick. The door gave slightly. A couple more should do it.

A bullet hit the doorframe, sending up a tiny shower of wooden shards. He threw himself face down on the floor as another bullet struck the wall where he had only moments ago stood.

From where he lay, the angle would be impossible for Soloman to get off a good shot. If he moved, however …

He heard a cackling laugh from below, a sound, which brought a chill to his very soul. The man was actually enjoying the killing.

The first bullet came through the wooden floor of the balcony inches from Cole's leg. Soloman was underneath, firing off shots in measured intervals, punctuating each shot with a burst of laughter.

'I'm gonna kill you, Cole. I should have killed you back in your house. Thought I had, but you is one tough old bird.' The lever worked. 'But now, your day of reckoning is nigh.' The hammer cocked. 'Goodbye old timer. Enjoy your time in hell.'

The rapport boomed through the saloon.

Cole winced, squeezing his eyes shut, waiting for the searing pain.

It never came.

The acrid smell of cordite hit his nostrils and he slowly released his breath. He waited, straining to hear Soloman moving below. But there was nothing. Taking his chance, he sat up and peered down into the saloon.

There, by the double swing doors stood Stone, the big Sharps in his hands.

Amy Childer steered her little buggy down Lawrenceville's main street, Stacey sitting beside her. There was a gaggle of bystanders outside the livery stable, women and men looking aghast, faces white as chalk.

'What's been going on?' Amy asked.

'Gunfight,' said one old woman. 'A stranger came and now they are all dead.'

'All?'

'Kestler,' said another, 'and that horrible Haynes. All of 'em dead.'

'Big fat one went in there and a young fella shot him dead.'

Amy turned her face towards the saloon and saw two men emerging, both tall, one dressed in buckskins. The 'big fat one' had to be Soloman. She thanked God for that. And for Kestler too. Now perhaps, if she could keep Stacey sober, she could make something of her life. Nodding to the tiny huddle of onlookers, she eased her little buggy into the street and away from the town deciding, there and then, never to return.

They tied up what remained of the stolen antiques to the back of a purloined mule. A buggy driven by a striking woman drew up. Cole doffed his hat.

'I've been told there was shooting.'

'Some,' said Cole. 'It's all over now.'

'I was wondering ... There was a man named Soloman. He's been terrorizing my husband and I. Was he ...?'

'Yes, ma'am. He won't be troubling you no more.' Cole frowned, gestured towards the man slumped next to her. 'Is that your husband?' She grunted. 'I was told Kestler sent someone out to kill him.'

'Yes. I knocked him down with the flat of a shovel.'

Cole laughed. 'I'm guessing that is the least he deserved. What you planning on doing now, ma'am?'

She shrugged. 'Getting as far away from here as possible. Start anew. It's gonna be hard, my husband being as he is.'

'Ma'am...' Cole went over to the mule and dipped inside one of the sacks. He brought something wrapped in thick canvas out and went over to the woman. He carefully opened up the wrapping and pressed a beautifully carved figure into her hand. 'This here is a Meissen figurine, all the way from

Germany. It was my daddy's and is probably worth more than this whole town put together. I reckon in San Francisco you could raise enough money for any kind of life you wanted.'

Mouth hanging open, a single tear rolling down her face, she looked deep into Cole's eyes. 'I couldn't … This is more than generous, but I couldn't…'

"Course you can,' he said with a smile and patted her hand. 'I've seen enough killing this day to make me sick to my stomach. This'll go some way in making it all seem worthwhile.'

He stepped away and watched her closely as, sniffing loudly, she carefully put the figurine in the back of the buggy and moved away.

'My oh my, that was a fine thing you did there, Mr Cole.'

'You think so?' asked Cole, raising a single eyebrow towards Stone. 'So was what you did for me.'

Stone smiled awkwardly.

They returned to their grisly work. The bodies they piled up in an open wagon and together they took it to the undertaker's, whose boarded-up store appeared deserted, but they left it there anyway.

Without a word, both men began their journey back home.

Cole rode, leaving his past behind him, the decision now made. The killing had to end. With Roose dead, everything he had known was gone.

Except for Maddie.

Maddie who had begged him not to go, who warned him she would not be there when he returned.

If he returned.

Before either of them did, however, they went to search for Roose.

For the last time, Cole used his old tracking skills and when they reached the place, Stone cried. Cole, in silence, dug the grave.

The town, as they trotted into Main Street later that day, looked much the same as it ever did. Passing the sheriff's office, they saw young Thurst pinning up a couple of wanted posters on the board outside. He looked at Cole over his shoulder and stopped. He turned. 'You found him?'

Cole nodded and turned his gaze towards the end of the street. 'I buried what was left of him.' Something caught in his throat and he reached for his canteen and took a large drink, wishing it was something stronger. 'I'm sure gonna miss him.' People were going about their daily business, shopping, conversing, passing the time of day. If he had a photograph of this place from a quarter of a century ago, it would look exactly the same. Except that back then Sterling Roose would be part of it. Cole thought about that for a moment before pushing it to the back of his mind. They had had a good run, better than most, and Cole always knew something like this would happen in the end. For men like Roose and he, that was how life ran its course.

'What happens now?'

Snapped out of his reverie, Cole looked at Thurst. 'Elect a new sheriff, I guess.'

'Oh.' Thurst turned his face to the ground. 'Mr Cole, I admired Mr Roose a good deal. I'm gonna miss him.'

'Me too, son. Me too.' He gestured towards the sign for Sheriff above the door. 'You would make a fine sheriff, Stone.'

Stone gaped. 'Mr Cole ... I don't think ...'

'Nonsense, son. I'll put your name forward. But for now,' he inched his horse away, 'I have something a little more pressing to see to.'

He flicked the reins and moved gently forward, wondering what he would find waiting for him back home.

Breaking into a canter, he left the town limits and headed in the direction of his large home. The one his father had put so much energy into building. Cole never truly appreciated how cold the house was, nor how it could be warmed by the love of a good woman. Now, even that was lost to him. He should have tried harder, begged her to stay. However, he did not. His foolish pride once more got in the way and now, he truly was alone.

He came over the rise and reined in his horse, heart banging so hard against his chest he thought it might burst out.

There, just inside the gate was her buggy. In the stable yard, the horse munching on something. Something tasty no doubt. Something the little mare would always have.

Because she was there.

Maddie had not left.

As if sensing his approach, she appeared on the porch, framed in the doorway, the sleeves of her dress rolled up, a bandana around her forehead to keep her flowing blonde hair out of her eyes. She stood with a bucket in one hand and a mop in the other. She set them both down, put her hands on her hips and, even from this distance, he saw the flash of her smile.

Flicking the reins, his heart swelling, Cole kicked his horse into a gallop and the grin on his face was broader than it had ever been before in his entire life.

Dear reader,

We hope you enjoyed reading *He Who Comes*. Please take a moment to leave a review in Amazon, even if it's a short one. Your opinion is important to us.

Discover more books by Stuart G. Yates at https://www.nextchapter.pub/authors/stuart-g-yates

Want to know when one of our books is free or discounted for Kindle? Join the newsletter at http://eepurl.com/bqqB3H

Best regards,

Stuart G. Yates and the Next Chapter Team

The story continues in:
The Hunter by Stuart G. Yates
To read the first chapter for free, please head to:
https://www.nextchapter.pub/books/the-hunter

Lightning Source UK Ltd.
Milton Keynes UK
UKHW020837151220
375245UK00012B/1269/J